HONEŸBIRD

The Trip of a Lifetime...

RAFAEL FRANCIS

Honeybird is a work of fiction. All names, characters, businesses, places, events and incidents in this novel are either the product of the author's imagination or used in a fictitious manner. Any resemblance to actual persons, living or dead, or actual events is purely coincidental.

The opinions, statements and experiences included in this novel do not reflect that of the author, nor their associates. This novel is not a guide and is not to be used as educational material. The author does not encourage or condone the use of illicit drugs and illegal substances or any criminal activity under any circumstances.

The included material may be considered inappropriate or offensive and may trigger sensitive readers. This book contains heavy drug use, coarse language, sexual activity and mild violence.

Most of the uncommon words, phrases and slang terms mentioned in this novel can be found in the GLOSSARY on pages 182-183.

TABLE OF CONTENTS

"The fear of death follows from the fear of life. A man who lives fully is prepared to die at any time."

—Mark Twain

Chapter 1

Honeybird Definition:

1. A small, <u>drab</u> African bird of the <u>honeyguide</u> family.

2. Someone with an overwhelming sense of <u>curiosity</u> for the <u>unknown,</u> and the will to accept the <u>risks</u> that coincide.

Weed. Relaxation of the body, a euphoric state of mind and a heavily humorous outlook on your surroundings. *Uncontrolled hilarity.* What isn't remotely amusing, is. The trees are greener, gold shines brighter and your friends are staring into each other's eyes as if lost in a telepathic trance. They've become kindred souls in a matter of twelve and a half minutes. You're sedated, but your blood likes it, and your nerves are tranquil. The auditory resonations are comforting. Time flies while you remain stagnant.

Booze. You're confident, and you're able to speak the mind that you previously could not. Anxiety is dampened, and being more talkative and approachable allows you to connect better with the people around you. A few more drinks and your reactions aren't only delayed, they're wildly misjudged. Too much and you'll throw up. Driving a car, you'll kill somebody. At some point, you're desperately clinging on to the kitchen bench at a house party, glaring at the half bottle of Pirate Water upon it, cursing at it for what it's done to you. You attempt to stand, before realising you've returned to the floor.

March 16th

It was around 3 a.m. and Johnny wasn't waking up. I began to wonder if he'd died and left me with Alexandra. I was hoping he'd awaken, not only to make sure he was alive, but to act as a diversion from the girl I'd been left in a tangle with during his absence. It was a house party, but everybody had cleared off. It came down to only the three of us and a few passed-out drunks scattered throughout the wallpapered hallway of the home. Alexandra leaned over with her squeaky leather jacket and ran her fingers through my chest hair—*Jesus Christ*, I thought, *I should've waxed or at least shaved it*. She'd easily mistake me for a silverback ape.

"I dunno how I'm gonna get home, Clarkie," Alexandra whispered drunkenly in my ear, only just learning of my name and already tinkering with the pronunciation.

Maybe the chest locks of hair were for the better. I didn't want the attraction from her. I didn't even remember being introduced to her. She was a kind girl, pleasant for sure. But the subtle hints for me to drop her home in this state of mind was simply a bridge too far. Aside from that, she had these colossal buck teeth that stood out like somebody holding two planks of plywood atop her face. *Okay*, maybe it was the gin that'd been highlighting her flaws, but I wasn't the cream of the crop, the belle of the ball *or* the spring chicken either. I remember thinking to myself that usually alcohol makes people appear *more* attractive, *more* appealing and less repulsive. I then realised I'd been staring at her gargantuan buck teeth for about eight seconds straight. I had to look away, suspecting that she was probably insecure about them as it were.

"How far's your place? We'll walk there!" I offered, hoping my kindness would pay off, hoping that she'd see me as a generous acquaintance, doing her a solid by escorting her home in the dead of night and hinting that we *weren't* going to end up in bed together. Besides, the last thing I'd want is to send her packing and something horrific happens to her on the street. The fault would be mine in that case. I wouldn't possess the brains to withstand the guilt.

"Two train rides and a few blocks," she said. "We have to stop at Aunt Jenny's to get the back door keys, so my parents wouldn't know I'm out. Then another train ride and a three-block walk."

Kindness is a sneaky, sly villain. It either pays off in full, or it nails you repeatedly like the town whore. I blame my incessant need to please people—to the point of it impeding my own life and having to live with the consequences of doing so. Johnny happened to wake up at the time with squinting eyes and Dorito dust residing in his trimmed, Arabian beard. To me, it sounded like a flock of angels, awakening in silk garments among the clouds and harmonising in a high-octave choir. To anybody else, it sounded like a puking burp and the release of some noxious, deadly gas that repelled anyone within a 20-metre radius. At last, he was awake, and so, my ticket to freedom. He'd either distract us to lead Alexandra to inevitably find another way home, or he'd set upon that journey with us, intent not to leave me alone with her and this unfortunate situation in which she'd become *my* responsibility. It seems drinking a fuck-tonne of booze rewards you with the relief of being left alone, while generosity, kindness and semi-sobriety punish you by having to spend the night getting somebody else home safe—somebody who lacked the responsibility to plan their way home before skolling more than a few cans of Somersby Cider on a low tolerance.

I shrugged. "Oh, what the hell?" I threw my arms round Alexandra and Johnny, tethering our newfound trio. "Who *doesn't* fancy a light stroll in the Devil's hour?" I looked over at Johnny.

Amid my wandering thoughts and new hope that I'd have him by my side for the remainder of the night, my heroic saviour had fallen fast asleep. Out like a light. A tease—*I must've spent too long thinking. Fuck.*

*

Half past five. Alexandra kissed me on the cheek and climbed into her window. It turned out that she didn't need her aunt's keys after all—her bedroom window was left open, which meant about an hour of that journey was lost in time for a set of keys she didn't need. I suspected she knew the window was an option but utilised the elongated journey to thieve more time from me. At this point, I was mostly sobered up and wondered why I spent my night, and morning, dropping this girl off. The main quest was to return Alexandra home safely, but maybe it would've proved more worthwhile and rewarding if I'd just succumbed to her obvious attempts of seduction. I could sense it hours before that she yearned to wake up with my loose light brown hairs on her pillow.

I took an alternative route home, walking the whole way—no buses, no trains. I thought it'd be quicker, but I hadn't counted on the mass of construction sites in my path. I ventured directly through because around would take at least another fifteen minutes. It was a particularly windy night, so I tied my hair up and made my way through the cracks, puddles and machines that were shut off until morning. The sound of dripping and clanging gates echoed in the yard. I tried to keep my wits about me and push the negative, intrusive thoughts out of my mind to reduce the paranoia of being stalked or attacked in the still of the night. I found myself with a decision to make. I either had to cross a nasty, murky puddle to reach the other side which would take roughly twenty seconds or travel *around* the scaffolding with a clear, but narrow path that'd take about a minute. Having quite a slim figure, I knew I'd make it around with ease. I tried to make the safe bet this time.

As I tiptoed my way around the scaffolding, a cosmic gust of wind blew vigorously through the yard at the exact same time that I noticed a ten-cent coin embedded in the dirt. I kneeled to inspect it, but was instead frightened by a loud crash directly ahead of me—a 2-metre-wide piece of thick sheet metal had fallen from the roof of the scaffolded structure. I was stunned, almost struck by this speeding material that had now impaled the ground I was to momentarily walk upon if I hadn't stopped to notice the copper-nickel coin. It had fallen silently but crashed with such force. I'd never have seen it coming. Every nerve ending ceased and every hair on my skin had shot up like a shock of electricity.

*

Two months earlier, I'd been working tirelessly on a journalistic piece I called 'The Grimm Future of Tennis' as a sample piece for my application to *Sports Daily*. They were reviewing candidates for a new job opening and I thought I might've been in with a shot at securing my own segment, considering the pleasure I take in documenting and explaining something I'm passionate about—even in brutal honesty, which I had prided myself on. My parents were away in Bali and left the place to me, so Johnny was over almost every night. We'd spend one night drinking or smoking pot, and the next night working tirelessly on our own essays, Johnny for university, and me, for the application. There had been only one night where we decided to do both.

"What would you do if your life had a time limit?" Johnny looked up from his laptop and closed it, stroking his beard in deep thought.

I shrugged, knowing this conversation had no way of concluding in the next thirty seconds, thus closing my laptop, too. "I think I'd simply want to enjoy life as much as I can, knowing it's coming to an end and do everything I can to learn about *why* we're here, *who* I am and *what* my purpose is on Earth."

Johnny raised an eyebrow. "Sounds like that's been loaded in the barrel for a while." He stood up, his tall, lanky figure stepping over me to snatch a cold can of rum and coke from the desk. "We're so caught up in the illusion that our lives are gonna last until we're like eighty-five. Imagine studying for six years and—bam!— hit by a car, food-poisoned, heart attack, cancer."

Johnny was serious, yet to open that can of Kraken. "You had no real chance to enjoy life or learn anything about yourself." He shook his head, staring my way with his bloodshot eyes before taking a final drag of the poorly rolled joint. "There are things I wanna try."

"Like what?" I asked, hoping he wouldn't mention any long walks on the beach.

He shrugged. "There're substances out there that we're yet to experience. I've read some staggering stories and honestly, I wouldn't wanna die without knowing what these things feel like."

I wasn't going to say I wasn't interested or curious; in fact, I'd conducted extensive research myself about the use of psychedelics and their impact on exploring and improving the psyche. But wanting to do these things, acquiring the substance and finding the right time to experience them are three extremely different things— and that's without mention of the legal implications.

Nevertheless, *the seed had been planted.*

*

Back to the construction yard and standing a metre from that jagged metal sheet, I was startled over the close call, and that conversation with Johnny came flooding back. *What was I doing with my life?* I could've died, and not only could my life had met a grisly end, but I would've died knowing nothing about myself, who I am and if I even enjoyed my time on this planet. I had no published works, no great achievements and most of all, Johnny was right: nobody knows how long they've left to live. Every wasted moment in our lives is a moment somebody else has taken advantage of. Clark Burrows needed his name stamped on *something,* and I knew just what that thing was.

I finally reached home at 7:38 a.m. The sun had already risen, and I had a new lease on life. Something about that walk changed me and encouraged me to cook up this absurd idea upon the number of thoughts that coursed through my brain during that fateful walk home. As I stared at that ten-cent coin in the palm of my hand, the new idea was to set off with Johnny to experience every accessible substance mankind could offer, document the effects as we encounter them and test the limits of the human brain to its full extent with only one rule: to only try everything *once*. The result could unlock my psyche to understand myself, possess written works based on something real and have a fucking fantastic time doing so. Little did I know how difficult a task it'd be and how fucked up this journey could really get. Some of the worst ideas are fabricated when one has too much time to ponder and contemplate. Looking back, maybe I should have walked through the puddle instead, maybe I should've avoided the construction site, maybe I shouldn't have walked Alexandra home at all—one ounce of kindness could have horrific consequences in the grand scheme of things.

I called Johnny the moment I got inside. He took a while to answer as he was probably nowhere near his phone, or deep in the pits of a horrendous hangover. The positive for me was, I'd been awake the entire night, which somehow worked in my favour to avoid that dreaded morning fever. However, I downed a couple aspirins—*get it before it gets me*. As I impatiently waited for Johnny to pick up the phone, it wasn't only a matter of informing him about these new ideas from my 'brush with death' epiphany. Obviously, this half-baked prospect could've waited for a better time to be pitched, but I had so many thoughts streaming, screeching and trampling through my brain that I needed to unload them onto somebody, whether they listened or not.

Johnny answered finally with a croaky tone. "Dude, it's fucking seven." I could picture his head dangling off the bed, speaking indirectly towards the phone on speaker mode.

"Hear me out. Hear me out. You and I. Drop everything. Travel. Try everything. Document everything we get our hands on. This is it." I spoke quickly through the excitement and the vast multitude of synapses, firing a relentless abundance of thoughts in such a short time span.

Johnny was confused. It turns out I explained the verbs but had avoided the nouns like leprosy. It was a once-in-a-lifetime idea. At the time, in our twenty-three years of life, we'd only had extensive experience with alcohol and occasionally marijuana. Both of which were easy to come by and widely available. We'd only had a taste of a few other kicks like popping cream chargers in balloons and getting doped off codeine tablets meant only for the use of killing pain. Nothing extreme. These experiences felt as pathetic as huffing glue in the school art class or sniffing permanent markers until your head was sent spinning, committing a mass genocide of your neuronic brain cells.

Johnny was all in. Maybe he was waiting for something, or *someone* to push him. He was the type of guy to jump at the thought of an idea and ponder the consequences later. He'd poke a twig at a Nile crocodile just for the pure rush of adrenaline and laugh about it when people call him Armless Joe a month later. Maybe that's the reason I pitched it to him, or maybe because he was the only poor bastard that'd agree to do something this brainless and irresponsible with me.

Chapter 2

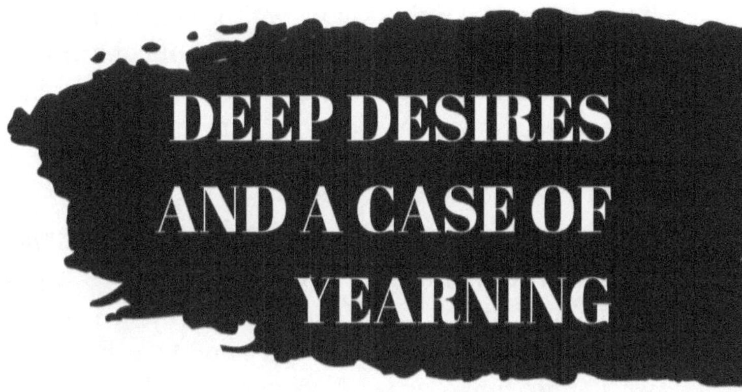

Before we set off on our merry way, we unfortunately had to wait a month and a bit. Johnny had to complete his degree in physics and after that, we were at a strange point in both our lives where we could blow a couple of months and do whatever the hell we wanted. This was the path I chose, and I wondered that if I let this opportunity slip by, we wouldn't ever have a chance of doing it again. Inevitably, Johnny would get a girlfriend, I'd get a job, or we'd simply grow too old and lose track of our hunger to endeavour upon these mindless, spontaneous escapades. The ticking of time was upon us and soon enough, we'd be so deeply rooted into our lives that we'd lack the capacity to try new things or experience new feelings. At that point, we may even disregard the fact that this would be a *good idea*, afraid that we'd grow older, develop narrow minds and witness the death of our curiosity. We had to take advantage of this rare opportunity in our lives where we didn't have any particular responsibilities or dependants. One of the motives for this journey was because I really didn't know who I was. I know I wasn't going to find it at the bottom of a bag of coke, but I heard enlightenment can be found in things like psychedelics and dissociatives. Which, in retrospect, *was a major understatement.*

At the time, I was between jobs. I had a gig at the local cafe on Blackburn Street. The manager was a prick as usual, his balding head and 'every young person is an entitled prick' attitude told the same tale. But this story isn't about him—*or is it?* Maybe I was living the life he wished he'd lived, rather than being forty-five and working a hospitality job he despised with customers fucking up his day by returning dishes and claiming there was "too much hollandaise sauce on my eggs benedict!". Either way, *fuck 'em.* I applied for that job in sports journalism and decided to quit the cafe. I was inspired by the recent Australian Open that took place earlier that year and my blazing desire to be in on the action—even if it meant from the sidelines. Who knew if I'd get the job? But the prospect of leaving that cafe was all too alluring. Whether I landed the position at *Sports Daily* or not, I was ecstatic to resign and wait for a response—giving me time to spread my wings between jobs with a fistful of savings and a friend to spend it with. I couldn't stand working a job that was beneath me when the expectation of a new position was such a step above—*maybe that's what Manager Baldy meant about being entitled?*

*

As Johnny's graduation approached, I decided to pack and set plans in motion for this unexpectedly massive voyage on which we were soon to embark. From Melbourne, we'd plan our journey and cruise to Sydney by car, then by plane we were to head to Queensland, whether it be Brisbane or the Gold Coast—*we hadn't decided that part yet.* Eventually, we wanted to get out of the country and stretch our legs, possibly start somewhere in Malaysia and let the whole thing play out naturally by impulse. In fact, we didn't want a solid schedule—we liked it better that way. *The unknown was all the more inviting.*

Leaving my family behind wasn't as tough a feat as I expected and surprisingly the more painless part of the process. My older brother was in Cambodia, building homes for the hungry in the struggling wastes and my parents were going through a rough patch in their marriage. We discovered that my father cheated on my mother before the wedding after the mistress contacted my mother out of spite to spill the beans. The incident was probably to blame for Charlie's spontaneous trip to Cambodia. My folks needed some time to sort out the sudden bombshell that had erupted into this massive awkwardness in my family. It also had me questioning what kind of man my father really was. *Maybe I needed this break, too.*

April 7th

Although I felt I was planning this trip for myself, Johnny was still on the phone with me nightly, plotting the blueprints of our adventure. Days before we made it official, I packed my clothes, shoes, belts, sunscreen, wallet, hats and toiletries in one duffle bag. The other duffle was simply more exciting, packed with four bags of weed—fresh off the plant and sun-dried by Carmen, a high school friend of mine who had the room to grow it beneath her house using hydroponics. The rest of the duffle was packed tightly with a small armoury of booze. Three sealed bottles of whisky, half a bottle of rum, half a bottle of gin and a fun-sized bottle of tequila. These additions weren't part of the overall journey; we simply referred to them as the 'in-betweeners'. Whether it meant going days without a new experience, we'd rely on the weed, or if it meant cutting a craving or an itch for any substance with addictive characteristics, the alcohol would remain as a pal to lean on. Johnny helped me jot up a list of drugs we wanted to get our hands on, experience and document.

As an aspiring journalist, my mantra was to *be different, be weird—or be cruelly forgotten.* Sport was my professional interest—far more accepted commercially— while substances drove my heart, or at least, my current state of interest and maturity. This journey wasn't objective, speculative journalism, but the intent was a personal experience from an uncorrupted origin. I'd like to think it was all academic, educational research and discovery—but the curiosity was the real drive, and the itching for a whole lot of fun in what would likely be the closing years of our youth, and of course, an open mind to potential self-discovery. Two things, we later learnt, were *vastly* different objectives.

The list consisted of a few things we'd never heard of at the time, and some that we probably weren't likely to get our hands on. Some of what we encountered weren't even part of that list—drugs we never even knew existed. Our initial scroll consisted of cocaine, LSD, morphine, ether, mescaline, magic mushrooms, peyote (at the time, we were unaware that peyote and mescaline were the same thing. Mescaline is simply the psychoactive compound extracted from peyote—but they both made the list, given our dangerous lack of knowledge) followed by ketamine, and finally, DMT which had always been on my bucket list: not the synthetic, crystalised lab version but the spiritual brew by the name of *ayahuasca*, only to be administered by a shaman in a traditional ritual.

Drugs. Everyone is intrigued by them. And if they aren't, they're simply uninterested in what the human brain can create and construct when subject to a compound that alters their perception of the world around them, or the internal happenings of their own consciousness. You'd be a fool not to be curious, but you'd be even more foolish to abuse these powerful, unpredictable substances. *Don't underestimate drugs.* If a tiny speck of paracetamol in a sugar-coated tablet can erase a gut-wrenching fever, a headache and a case of the sweats, imagine what an injection direct to the bloodstream can do—better yet, a toxic deliriant of most wicked and evil capability. We originally agreed on naming this endeavour and the resulting piece of documentation *The Trip of a Lifetime*—a clever play on words to reflect our thrill-seeking inclinations.

    With less than a week before our departure, Johnny had a friend at his university who had connections to this *other* guy who had leftover acid tabs in his possession: LSD. This was a big check off our list and the first step in crossing items off that list. LSD is also quite accessible if you know the right people—and it doesn't hurt the wallet as much as you'd initially think. *Don't fret*, I'm not leaving you in the lurch—these substances are explained as we experience them. After all, that's what this book is all about. And don't take this as any kind of guide—I do not condone or encourage the use of drugs to *anybody*. It is exclusively your choice and your risk. Most, if not *all*, of these drugs are illegal in most countries and potentially deadly if misused. This is only a journal of my own, personal experiences from a standpoint of being without any real past trauma or mental/medical conditions—that I know of. *A fresh slate ... so buckle in.*

Chapter 3

Johnny was able to get a hold of six tabs of acid. They're presented on small pieces of blotter paper, usually squares, smaller than your fingertip. LSD could also be referred to as Blotters, Boomers, Trips, Dots and Lucy—and sometimes distributed in microdots or liquid form. Six tabs were far more than required for a couple of beginner trippers. Lysergic Acid Diethylamide. Extracted from ergot, it's a type of fungus that infects rye (grains), and the psychoactive properties are hallucinogenic. Psychedelics have always piqued my interest, even though I'd never really dabbled with them in any way before. The closest I had come was nangs, and even *they* are classified as dissociatives, and only last about five to twenty seconds in small bursts, and still, they hadn't reached the heights of my brain constructing visuals from thin air.

The first and only experience with cream chargers I had was at a simple house party. Some Kiwi guy grabbed a six-pack of Mercury ciders and closed the fridge door as I inhaled a green, pre-filled balloon in the centre of the kitchen. Somebody had assured me beforehand that it should only make me feel a little more drunk ... *and then the soundwaves stretched.* It was as if I'd excessively expanded an audio file on my brain's computer. My movement was slowed and my eyesight heavily delayed—suddenly I had some random Asian girl, who I'd never met before, walk past and look at me strange.

"Is this your first time on *nangs?*" She giggled, tilting her head and standing unbearably close to my face.

I nodded, slightly disorientated and unable to speak for a few seconds before the effects soon wore off. It seems everybody knew what nangs were and you couldn't blame them—they're far too accessible and so affordable that even the companies selling these whipped-cream chargers know for a fact that about fifty to sixty percent of their worldwide sales weren't for the basic use of whipping cream, but utilised to get fucked off your brains for a matter of about ten seconds on average. They make exceptional profits, *so why stop manufacturing?*

Nangs are distributed in steel cylinders filled with nitrous oxide—about the size of a small index finger. They're cracked open in a number of ways and are released into some kind of balloon to contain the gas. You inhale slowly, then exhale back into the balloon without taking in any oxygen apart from whatever's inside that balloon. The less oxygen in your lungs before inhalation always makes for a heavier effect. The nitrous oxide acts as the oxygen that your body attempts to live off—therefore cutting air from your brain and replacing it with nitro, forcing your central nervous system to relay and exchange information with substantial delay and distort your perception of reality very temporarily. Inhalation is always the express way to the brain aside from intravenous injection. This comes as a kick, but I've never been sold on being a regular user of nangs for two reasons. First off, it's an embarrassingly cheap drug that's laughed upon and almost—like I mentioned earlier—comparable to huffing glue. Secondly, cutting your brain's access to oxygen is never an intelligent thing to do, especially by means of replacing it with something of a greater danger, and *especially* when the kick only lasts long enough to readjust your balls.

April 21st

Johnny and I waltzed into the casino and spent an hour or two taking in the dazzling lights and bustling scenery, occasionally ordering unique cocktails with odd names like the Anna Banana, the Coco Loco and April Rain. Sitting at a corner cocktail table at the sports bar, watching Manchester United's public shaming by Sevilla at 2–0 on the big screen, the alcohol started to wear off and we'd spent far above our quota for the night. Booze is ridiculously costly in Australia. A 700ml JD bourbon would set you back a cool sixty bucks. In Europe, it'd be less than half that price. Johnny and I made a pact that night at the bar as we watched yet another goal conceded by Man U. We agreed that we'll drink only from our stash of pre-purchased booze on the domestic part of this trip and save the binge drinking for overseas. It saves funds and gives us some fire to look forward to—especially if we were to hit a dull patch somewhere down the road.

Johnny whipped out the tabs on a secluded table. "One now, and one later."

"You've gone *loony*." I shook my head, scanning the room in case someone was wise. "I heard one tab takes you the distance, especially for a first time, and to mix two with alcohol would be far too unpredictable, especially smack-bang in the centre of a bustling casino."

It did tempt me, though. As much as I liked to think of myself as the voice of reason, the thought of buzzing sounds and flashing lights on a trip pressed my mouth to salivate. Little did I know that, unlike the dice on those tables, the casino probably wasn't the safest place to be rolling, especially for the first time. *One tab would prove plenty.*

"Only one," I said. "Let's not die before we start this journey."

Johnny reluctantly agreed before explaining where his friend got the acid. Shaun, this skinny eighteen-year-old friend of Johnny's: he had this egg-shaped head with a few strands of hair sticking up from it, kind of like Daffy Duck, and he sounded a little like him too. He had the tabs left to him at a party and didn't know what to do with them until the opportunity came along to offload them onto Johnny so his parents wouldn't find them during their weekly rummaging. It all seemed fine and dandy, but Johnny didn't bother asking how long Shaun had these tabs for, or how they've been stored. He'd simply been too excited, took them off his hands and wished Shaun a jolly weekend. We wondered whether it was worth taking to the bathrooms to place the tabs on our tongues like a typical, seasoned junkie would—but after a quiet, yet meticulous discussion, we agreed it takes half a second to sublingually administrate a tab at a table in the corner of the bar. Johnny laughed, placing the tab under his tongue, excited for the rush. I was also surging with anticipation, but being me, I had the fear in the back of my mind—the fear of a bad trip, especially considering the location and the possibility of these blotters being expired, if that was even possible. A mental state of fear, anxiety or any kind of depressed thoughts—or *anything* negative, for that matter—usually means you should steer clear of any psychedelics, or general drugs, in *any* situation.

Set and setting are the most important factors when taking something that alters your mind. 'Set' means mindset. *Are you in a good mood, content with yourself and in a good place in your life?* Anything and everything may and probably will get in your way. This ranges from current relationships, self-hatred, the effects of past trauma, your financial stresses and any mental pressure you're enduring at all. A good state of mind is the first step to a bearable trip. This may not guarantee a good trip because your brain might surface those negative, intrusive thoughts and your deepest, darkest secrets and insecurities anyway (which may not be a bad thing during a period of self-discovery) but it'll definitely steer you in the right direction to avoid it in the simple endeavour of having a good experience.

'Setting' is your environment, the people around you and the location you're taking these substances in. This really depends on the drug in question, but you never want to be somewhere uncomfortable or in a place that doesn't suit the substance. For example, you wouldn't want to be neck deep in the closed-eye visuals of a 5-MeO-DMT trip in the middle of a nightclub. In contrast, you wouldn't really take any uppers when you're alone in your apartment with no music and virtually no outlet for the raw energy it brings on. Additionally, the people around you can greatly affect a trip. You want to be around people that you're comfortable with. Not just people you like. These need to be trustworthy folk who know who you are, how you react to stressful, pressurised situations, what your past experiences are and especially people that won't get you into any kind of trouble. Paranoia during the come up, or during the trip, can absolutely obliterate your experience—or even send you into some kind of psychosis at higher doses.

Johnny tapped his fingers, impatiently waiting for it to kick in. As I mentioned before, this was no mere nang. LSD was a major game-changer for us, *big-boy shit*, and at the time, easily the heaviest substance in the drug-iverse that we'd taken so far and quite the jump from weed and booze.

Our expectation was an instant effect, and after about a half hour sitting at the bar and watching the Europa League post-game conferences, Johnny shrugged with a lazy lower lip.

"They've gotta be expired, man," he sighed, having acquired the blotters off Shaun when he probably hadn't stored them correctly because he likely had no clue how.

I quickly ran a search—I didn't like doing this. Our aim was to experience every substance we could get our hands on without knowing exactly what to expect, to chase a more fulfilling high—only understanding it with very basic knowledge of how much to dose and what it does to you in simple terms. *It was all the thrill of the game.* We learned that for LSD blotter paper to retain its potency and prolong its shelf life, it must be stored in the dark, away from hot temperatures and in an opaque container of some kind, preferably wrapped in tin foil since it evaporates far quicker than water. The ultraviolet rays cause it to break down at rapid rates. I didn't bother searching anything else because I wanted to save the unknowing thrill for a time where it actually worked.

We began walking through the slot machines, hoping to pull a few levers on the way out when I noticed something from the corner of my eye. A flicker, some kind of shimmering diamond. I spun to see what it was, but my vision didn't follow the same pace as my brain. My nerves felt disconnected. When I realised that the drug had taken hold out of absolutely nowhere, I panicked, thinking the expired substance was doing a number on us in the worst way and in the worst possible place. The acid had finally kicked in like a steam train running at 170 kilometres per hour. I took a glance over to Johnny, who was already hanging on to the back of a chair that somebody was sitting on at the slots. *I* saw that it was acid, although regular casino-goers would assume drunkenness. Disorientated, he looked back at me, blinking quickly as if he'd been hit by an even larger invisible locomotive. I began to wonder if we'd been dropped at the exact same time, in sync, or if I was simply too delayed to notice a change in his attitude until I looked in his direction. For all I knew, he could've been stumbling for the past five minutes beforehand, yet somehow, we were still within arm's reach.

Everything in sight was wobbling, swaying. I was about to speak to Johnny when I heard a woman laugh—but it was more of a giggle and for some reason, that giggle repeated itself three times back to me as if it were played on a recorded loop. My mind was warped, merging all the colours of the casino into one big spiral in front of me. *Yes, a spiral*—the typical depiction of kaleidoscopic drugs in the sixties. It was almost exactly as described in representations and visualisations. I closed my eyes, but it only made matters worse. The sounds heightened and rippled as if I were a blind man, and those helixes followed me and rendezvoused beneath my eyelids, corkscrewing even further out of control as if it had spread to the dancing phosphenes on my eyes. I began to wonder if we'd taken this drug in the wrong place, and that these overwhelming senses, visual and auditory hallucinations may have been more euphoric and comforting in a safer, quieter space.

Inexperienced to the duration of the effects of LSD, we roamed the casino for hours, stopping at every poster, every sign and every patterned floor. Never before had we been so mesmerisingly enticed by these intricate designs and shapes. Simple, yet so astronomically complex. We managed to ride this trip out until about 8 a.m. the next morning, having wandered through the shopping mall and its closed stores and food courts for hours, eventually finding ourselves comfortably resting in massage chairs in one of those pop-up shops in the middle of the complex. I remember staying overly conscious of mirrors and the need to avoid them, as I'd previously been informed that acid and reflective glass *do not* mix. There's always a chance you'll see your face melt or tear apart in front of your very eyes, or your deepest insecurities dramatised and blown out of proportion—for me, that'd be my self-consciously large nose growing four times the size and drooping like honey from a dipper— the idea of anything like that sickened me and scared the living shit out of me.

After the sleepless night and our senses that then seemed dull and mundane, we'd somehow forgotten that we had booked a room in the tower that night, but never checked in: $219 down the shitter and a spotless room for the casino to leave in wait of the next guests—*the house wins again*, yet this time, in an unusual way. The comedown consisted of mild nausea and a lengthy bathroom sitting. I'd say constipation, but I really couldn't blame that on the drug as it could've simply been due to my stubborn diet at the time, consisting of nothing but two-minute noodles and a bag of chips every now and then.

Johnny had it worse. He described his trip as an intense experience of flying colours and mentioned that at one point, everybody in the casino began screaming in unison—I'd forgotten whether he described that as an auditory experience or a visual; either way, it was strange. His comedown was also different. He hadn't thrown up, but he mentioned an acute front-of-forehead headache—

only finding relief when lying down. As we packed our bags at Johnny's place before setting off to Sydney, I noticed only *three* tabs remained. Our plan was to get rid of them or sell them somewhere down the road, but I distinctly remembered him purchasing six from Shaun. At that point, he admitted that he'd taken a second tab after we left the sports bar, thinking the first one was too weak to set in, assuming it was expired regarding the lack of effect, possibly explaining the heightened intensity and distressed experience he endured. If this was any indication of what to expect from Johnny's impulsive spontaneity over the coming months ... *we were in for some serious shit.*

Chapter 4

Sydney was elected as our next location, not for its popularity, or the harbour or the Opera House. It was the connections and what we could get our hands on when we arrived, and it just happened to be in the direction of our travels upon eventually reaching Southeast Asia. After Johnny provided the LSD, I knew it was my turn to send us on our next trip. I knew a girl named Fritz—it was her surname and for some reason back in school, we'd call everybody by their surnames, so much, that I'd frequently forget her *given* name: Beth. After she moved to Sydney, we began chatting online and eventually the conversation led to substances. She persistently jabbed at me to visit her in Sydney one day and threatened to 'corrupt' me with a happy pill. Although it intrigued me, I never had the opportunity, nor the yearning to actually make the journey to meet her. *Travelling over 700 kilometres for some molly? I think not.* And one part that I was afraid of was that she seemed interested in more than just sharing a baggie of caps.

Johnny and I took turns driving my rusty burgundy hatchback all the way to Sydney—*small car, but a monster of a thing round the bends*—we accumulated about five and a half hours of driving each. At one point, I was forced to pull over and have Johnny pilot the car after catching a flicker in my eye, reminiscent of the glistening diamond I experienced on acid at the casino. They say acid stays in your body for up to three days after consumption and is broken down quickly so it can't be detected on a drug test, but many say that once you ingest LSD, it's in your body forever, and forevermore a part of you. The phenomenon I had experienced in the car is referred to as a flashback: *Hallucinogen Persisting Perception Disorder (HPPD)*. These are said to be lasting visions and potential cases of micropsia that linger for a certain time frame after taking LSD or any range of other psychedelics. It could reveal itself within days after consumption, or from weeks, to months and sometimes years, or in most cases—never at all. We've also heard horror stories of users being *perma-fried* by a heavy acid dose or constant abuse, sending you into an undying hallucinatory state—permanently reduced cognition. In basic terms: an *eternal nightmare*, sentenced to trip for the rest of your fucking life.

May 3rd

Reaching a cafe in Sydney, I spent a good hour alone with Johnny because I had a hunch that we wouldn't be one-on-one for quite a while. Fritz was a party girl and even if the Earth came to a complete halt—*she'd still be spinning.*

"Just warning you, Fritz is a little over the top." I sighed as the waiter placed our much-craved coffees in front of us. "And it's likely that when we catch up with her, she's probably not going to leave us alone until we book it outta here."

"Dude." Johnny laughed with a headshake. "She clearly wants to get you into bed if she's *that* keen for you to come here."

I didn't agree with him, but I also hadn't disagreed. It seemed odd that someone from another state was constantly offering me pingers and a ton of other crap in exchange for a casual visit. However, we had a set goal. Anything we had to do for it was simply part of the task and sometimes sacrifices would inevitably need to be made. If ecstasy was the next drug on the list and Fritz would provide it upon having to pash for a couple of minutes, then so be it—*everyone wins.*

With her fiery red hair, painted-on freckles and shin-high Doc Martins, Fritz was the definition of a party animal. A shapeshifter, fitting in with any crowd. She was what Johnny and I had in mind when it came to living *la vida loca.* Upon meeting at her apartment in Kings Cross, Johnny and I had a few drinks to down during her time getting ready. A couple of cold pale ales.

"Make yourselves at home!" Fritz only wore a bra, underwear and socks as she made her way to the vanity mirror with a stick of eyeliner. "You don't mind if I walk around in this, do you?"

I couldn't help but notice Johnny's wandering eyes every now and then. It also made me question if I'd been fooled by her flirtatious tendencies, misinterpreting her interest in me. She seemed to be a natural seductress. Maybe she was just extrovertedly affectionate with every entity she came across. As she slipped on a stretchy pink skirt, she handed both Johnny and I a pill each. These pills were pink with a warped smiley face stamped upon them.

"Let's have us a ferocious night, fellas," Fritz said excitedly. "We're headed to The Cliff Dive. I've got a friend who works there and a drink card with my name on it."

I realised she probably hadn't had any kind of romantic or sexual intention, which was a relief knowing she hadn't invited us there with an ulterior motive.

I tapped her on the shoulder, turning down the raving music. "How much do I owe ya for this?" I whispered. "I don't take free handouts."

She turned around, raised her eyebrow and laughed in my face. "All I ask is you get along with my friends," she said as she lit a long, skinny pre-rolled smoke, sliding it between her glossed lips. "Can you manage that?"

Gosh darn, I'm not going to lie—her temperament was far sexier than I remembered.

In my experience, you'll only have good quality shit if it's free from a trusted friend—or if you pay big bucks for it. But either way, there's always that 'grey area' risk that the drug—especially pills and lab drugs—may never be exactly what you think you've purchased. And those dealers might even jack up their prices to make you think you're buying pure, high-grade-quality shit when it's probably cut with a heap of different chemicals and other cheaper, dangerously lower-grade additives.

We were ready to down the pills with a swig of ale before we heard a loud thumping on her door. Fritz seemed wildly exhilarated by it, skipping to the front of the apartment.

I whispered to Johnny. "Should we save it? We don't really know these people."

I glanced at Johnny's open palm. It was empty. He'd already popped it with a smirk.

"Fuck it," I said, downing it with a swig of beer before two girls and a gay guy strutted into the apartment. *Who knows who could've waltzed through that door?* You're forced to expect the literal worst with these things, knowing how fragile the experience could be amid bad company.

Korey was his name, wearing a blue striped shirt and carrying a stylish fake-leather satchel. The other two girls were Zoe and Paige. Annoyingly enough, Korey gave off this cock-blockingly obnoxious energy that drove Johnny and I up the wall. He initially referred to me as Mark. He must've misheard it, and thanks to my inability to correct him, I let him assume that *Mark* was indeed my name. It would've been far too embarrassing for the both of us if I'd corrected him after the twenty-third time of him saying it.

While Fritz spent about an eternity picking out a pair of shoes, Paige was scrolling Johnny's phone. "Alternative rock is the good stuff," Johnny advised. "Give it a listen. It's a rabbit-hole. I've got three playlists

I usually listen to—"

"Fuck that shit!" Korey snatched the phone. "I wanna get hyped, bitches! I don't wanna be in my *feeels*." He switched the music to some sped-up version of modern trance music, deliberately plunging himself on the couch between Johnny and Paige.

I smirked at Johnny as he slouched into the leather beneath him with a shrug, finishing his beer. Either way, it was strange because we had no initial interest in these women, nor they in us. Regardless, it seemed Fritz had a big night prepared, and we were only just getting started.

MDMA, MD, Ecstasy, Eckies, Caps, E, Pingers, Flippers, Molly—whatever the fuck you want to call it, they're all just slang terms for Methylenedioxymethamphetamine. After trying to sound out or read that word aloud for the first time, or even in your head, it quickly makes sense why there are such numerous slang terms for it. The twenty-nine-letter word is so long that you'd almost be on the comedown before you've finished sounding it out. MDMA is a little more of a risk to your health. Fillers and other chemicals can be mixed in with the drug and some pills you might come across may not even contain that massive word mentioned above, potentially causing a bad experience with an array of negative side effects. It's supposed to make you feel happy, accepted and comfortable with yourself and your surroundings—an empathogen, originally manufactured to treat PTSD and other mental health conditions such as anxiety, depression and eating disorders. But in some cases, it's known for the exact opposite and can even cause mild hallucinations in higher doses. Some call it an investment—as if you're borrowing the happiness of tomorrow and doubling down on it tonight. The comedown—being a real kick in the teeth—could potentially lead to weeks, and sometimes months of depressed, or even suicidal, thoughts in severe cases on account of missing the raw positive energy on the drug and the overdriven serotonin receptors in the body.

We reached the club and for me, I already stumbled in on the wrong foot.

I nudged Johnny, "Dude ... I forgot my ID."

"You're kidding—they might not let you in." Johnny chewed his lip. "Just act mature."

Waiting in the entry line, I was paranoid of being sent away, especially when it meant ruining the night of our newfound acquaintances, or Johnny's, for that matter. The last thing you want is to be left out on the street when rolling on caps. Every step closer to the bouncer introduced another bead of sweat on my forehead. I was in a panic of nerves and anxiety. I worried my friends would head inside without me due to the dumb mistake of forgetting that piece of plastic that gets you into nightclubs. The heavy, bald bouncer was checking IDs. He had a Scottish accent.

"ID." He carefully checked over Fritz's. "Yep." He directed her inside.

"ID, mate?" He asked for Korey's.

Korey acted overly flattered at the basic question. "Thanks, Doll Face. Still got a couple o' years left in me!" To which the bouncer rolled his eyes.

The bouncer glanced over me, Johnny, Paige and Zoe before allowing us entry. Relief flushed over my face. I wondered if Korey's irritating remark had given the bouncer just about enough to be done with our group. As we entered, I could feel the music rumbling through my veins. Perhaps the ecstasy was rolling in. My heart was still beating fast after the close encounter with that bouncer—after-effects of anxiety lingered for a short period of time before an invitingly warm feeling embraced my stomach. I looked over at Johnny, and his eyes widened. I knew he was feeling the same sensation. I started doing The Robot for some reason and I remember Johnny finding it extremely hilarious— watching my comical moves break the tension among an ever so serious crowd. *For sure*, I thought, *we're in Molly's grip.*

After a few Jager bombs and tequila shots, I had begun feeling something euphoric. I wanted to talk to somebody, ignite a conversation. I felt I had a billion things to say and all I needed was somebody to listen. The tingling nerves began, up and down my body—they were oddly pleasant. My fingers were starting to feel warm and soft. I felt as if a heavy physical weight had been lifted off my shoulders—*effortless motion, as if I could perform ballet with ease.* I glanced over to Fritz to give her the nod to let her know that it's kicked in, but it hit me. There was something about her in that moment of time. She was a red-head—I'd never been into red-heads or had any history of crushing on a red-head—but as she danced, the sweat on her skin was an extension of her. A pure embodiment of her exhilaration and connection with the music. It struck me when she raised her arm to shift her hair out of her face. It was as if time slowed for a second, as if I'd spent fifteen minutes watching this one action take place.

The strobe lights were causing her to flicker in and out of my vision in slow motion—with every flash of light, her body would sway a different way. She closed her eyes after shifting her hair, caught in the moment. The red strands were left messy atop her head but something about it was unbearably breathtaking. I wanted to hold her, connect with her, tell her how stunningly pretty and irresistibly gorgeous she was, even though in sobriety, I knew for a fact that I wasn't crazy about her, or felt the need to tell her that. But I wanted to, not only for myself but I wanted her to feel good, valued and flattered—she deserved it. *She's such a fucking beautiful person.* Everything seemed right, perfect, balanced and happy. I wanted to embrace her and share that sense of joy with anybody else I could connect with. *This stuff is magic.* It was a kind of new love. I've felt love before, a few times. But this wasn't the basic emotion of romantic interest. It was more, something more powerful, something indescribably enchanting. A love of another realm materialised from nothingness, knowing no bounds.

I began to make my way to her, except in the back of my mind, I wondered if this move might cause her to think I'm leading her on when we were sober again. *It didn't stop me.* I ordered a drink for her and myself and noticed Johnny dancing with Korey in the distance. I laughed, thinking maybe Johnny gave Korey the wrong idea. I left that part up to them. I was suddenly drenched in sweat—but it felt strange on my skin as if it were silky and slimy. Walking back through the crowd, I was peaking at this point and wanting to embrace Fritz so badly to the point of crushing her in my arms—I noticed *her* own arms wrapped around somebody else. I stopped, realising later that these feelings on MDMA can be felt for anybody you're focused on, and through her perspective, that obviously meant somebody else. She kissed him and he grasped her waist. He was much taller, more handsome than I. My blood ran quick, and my heartbeat heightened. It wasn't jealousy. I couldn't explain it. Maybe the love I had to give couldn't be expressed the way it wanted to because she was occupied.

Some remixed version of 'Come on Eileen' started playing and the strings at the beginning of the song were unbearably tuned higher in pitch, screeching and resonating into the cavities of my ears. I glared at the DJ from afar as if he'd deviously tuned it that way just to fuck with me. I soon realised how ridiculous that accusation would sound. The back of my ears warmed and I began to feel uneasy. My surroundings began closing in and I felt that I couldn't breathe. I was trapped in some kind of visual and auditory manifestation of pure anxiety. I looked around and every voice was louder, so loud that I couldn't understand what they were saying. I stared at my hands, noticing the cracks within my palms being ultra-focused and highly detailed, as if it were a close-up view of a dried-up desert. I turned away, focusing on something else before my consciousness was to be sucked into the trenches of my palm. If this was the true peak, I was in the wrong mindset for it. I rushed through the crowd, past Fritz, Johnny and Korey to the bathroom and my heart was beating faster than it'd ever pounded before. *Holy shit. Holy shit!* I could only breathe in, not out. *Fuck.* I looked around, desperate for hydration. My heart was skipping beats, working too hard to process the terrorising anxiety among whatever unknown chemicals had been streaking through my veins. I looked into the mirror in sheer panic. I could see my heart literally beating out of my chest. *I'm going to have a fucking heart attack.* The veins were popping from my forehead and temple. *I'm not going to make it out of here.* My pupils grew larger and wider, overlapping the whites of my eyes as I desperately held myself up on the vanity. *I'm going to die in the bathroom of a fucking nightclub.* My jaw hung with a lack of control. I turned from the mirror, knowing the reflection was only intensifying my paranoia. The light-headedness was streaming in, and I was struggling to maintain my equilibrium. A group of boys in sweaty Bintang singlets entered, raving and squawking.

I felt one of them touch my shoulder, "You all good, bro?"

I tried to speak but my chest couldn't push out the words because it had been thumping excessively. I needed to escape. I slowly navigated my way back to the dance floor, step by step to avoid aggravation of my imminently imploding cardiovascular system. I stepped slowly through the jumping crowd as if it were water—surely, the DJ had been ripping a banger at the time, but to me it was just noise. I finally reached the corner of the club, crouching with my eyes closed. Tears were helplessly running down my cheeks. The overwhelming chemical reactions in my brain needed an outlet. With my eyes closed, the music grew louder, the vibrations were pumping hard against me, the other guests' voices were drowning every gap I had in my audible threshold. The more I shut my eyes, the more the anxiety and paranoia overcame me. *Everybody's staring at me, wondering what the hell I'm doing curled up in the corner.* I took a deep breath, controlling my inhales and exhales, holding the one piece of fabric that was my shirt and its surprisingly pleasant feel in my hand—the only comforting thing I could grab hold of. I was worried they'd call the police or the security to kick this whacked-out junkie out of the club. I wished I'd just open my eyes in my quiet bedroom, alone.

"Clark. The car's out front." I heard Johnny's muffled voice slicing through the mess of music. "They're waiting on us." The most relieving words I could hear in a situation like that.

In the back of a car beside Johnny, staring out the window at all the flashing city lights go by, I could've sworn I'd seen a naked man running alongside the vehicle at some point, but who's to say if my brain was simply well overworked. I was just thankful that we were on the way home, and that I could finally get some rest. My heart rate dampened, and so did the anxiety.

The rumours were true. The next morning, I woke with a piercing headache and threw up as soon as I got out of bed, feeling below the standard of *shit*, as if all the toxicity inside me was wallowing in the trenches of my gut, lurking and waiting for a vertical movement to release itself. Although, it could've been the alcohol on account of the lack of water I consumed. I spent half the day in the bath, then the other half in bed. Johnny had that same front-of-forehead headache that he felt after the LSD comedown, but this time he said it pained a little more.

MDMA is a cruel motherfucker. I sat there for about three days in regret over that one dose while Johnny was already out drunk with Fritz two nights in a row after. It was true about the investment—about using tomorrow's happiness to double down on tonight. But for me, it used the happiness from three days, and sent my night into hyperdrive, turning that happy investment into a nightmare. Somehow, I experienced both sides of the drug, but about eighty percent of the night was swallowed by the negative. It had me guessing whether it was true MDMA or something else.

Chapter 5

LOVE AND OTHER FUCKED-UP CHEMICALS

After about a week hibernating in Fritz's apartment, I had a few cold ones with Johnny and Zoe. Zoe was one of Fritz's best girls and she was there on the night at The Cliff Dive. She had straight black hair and a button nose with a flick on the end of it. Her most discernible feature would be her silver eyebrow piercing—I never was a fan of those things until I met her. I initially found her somewhat attractive, but we never really exchanged words until the second week of the Sydney stay. We were playing billiards and Zoe plain sucked, although I found it amusing and she did too. That gave me the licence to tease her for it, especially for the fact that her height limited her reach on the table, being considerably the shortest of all her friends.

"Don't distract me." She bit her tongue with a smirk. "I don't practise as much as I should."

I watched her from the opposite side of the table, lining up a shot with heavy focus on the white ball. Zoe had these radiant, brown eyes. They'd swallow you the more you looked into them. Eye contact is pivotal for human connection. The strongest attraction to a human being is when the bond is made *after* the initial introduction—unbiased of looks, but upon judgement of a likeable personality that compliments the physical aspects, resulting in an increased material attraction.

"I knew you'd have a bad trip. I could sense it." She smiled, sincere. "I hope I'm not overstepping but I've been there many times. I know it's not fun."

"I don't know what went wrong. Everybody else seemed fine." I shrugged, chalking my cue. "Is it possible I got a bad batch?"

Zoe laughed. "Nah, Beth gets it from our mate, Jetty. He's quality."

"So, I was the problem?" I smirked with an eye roll.

"I remember you forgot your ID. And you looked *so* worried. That's bound to set off a bit o' paranoia. It was an unsettling situation and when you're coming up, it follows you into the trip." I cracked open another can of Scotch and coke, setting the balls up for a break. "I know what you guys are doing here." Zoe grinned, leaning on the pool table. "Fritz told me."

"She made me look stupid, didn't she?" I clenched my teeth.

Zoe looked to the ceiling with a shrug, "Did she make you look *stupid?* No. Is it a stupid idea? Possibly." She chuckled.

I sighed with a smile. "I know, I know. It's preposterous but—"

"No. The journey you're on might be quite beneficial. Some travelling and some life experience and introspection never hurt nobody." Zoe sat down with her arms and legs crossed on the couch.

It was the first time I could make out her tattoos. They looked meaningful, unlike the usual snakes, butterflies and roses that I'd already noticed printed along the arms of Fritz. These were different, unique. She had subtle hydrangeas on her forearm, angel wings and Aztec art down her legs—*no colour*, which I favoured. I reminded myself to ask about them later, maybe even as a conversation starter.

"I've tried an array of shit—*believe it or not*," Zoe continued. "So, take it from me. You're *not* gonna get too far if you keep your defences so high."

"What do you mean?" I said after shooting the break. "We *must* have our wits about us on this shit."

She nodded, parting her hair from her face. "By defences I mean intrusive, insecure thoughts and paranoia." She stood up to grab the pool cue. "Those factors could control your trip, and completely ruin it. On good drugs, you need to not care what people think. You need to let it envelop you. If you've taken a sensible dose, just lean into it—you'll come out the other side."

I smiled. It was the advice I needed, and it came at a good time, early in our journey. She continued. "'Cause if you're gonna die on a trip, you're gonna die. Paranoia and bad thoughts only make it worse. May as well enjoy your last minutes. Right?"

She smiled as I cracked up. "That's dark ... but you're not wrong."

Zoe was growing on me. The only issue here was, after my bout with ecstasy, I developed an everlasting attraction to Fritz, where there were no feelings before. The initial desirability was purely physical upon our arrival, but this was more than that. She occupied my mind day and night. I couldn't help thinking, imagining and fantasising about her. The beads of sweat on her chest, her legs brushing on the silk sheets, my inhales and her exhales in total and complete synchronisation, the contraction of her facial muscles while her red fingernails claw the pillows—*stop it at once. This isn't healthy.* Maybe this was only of a lustful nature—which was hopeful, but in no way normal to me. I didn't think I'd find such attraction in something I was never drawn to before. Some may say this symptom is impossible on the drug, and that you love and talk to *everybody* when on it—well, it happened to me and that's how I felt. *Who knows?* MDMA is also known to have lasting effects. You could be left weeks with an afterglow, which leaves you with an enlightened, more confident outlook on life in general, or like I said about the comedown—the complete opposite.

I spent the next week with Zoe, every single day to the point where we'd talk about our substance experiences and how her priorities were the absolute opposite to mine. She wasn't a fan of ecstasy, and she'd only tried cocaine once. What she *had* dabbled in was shrooms and peyote—*psilocybin and mescaline* in chemical compound terms. She was a fan of psychedelics and at the time, was microdosing shrooms weekly to enhance her mood and boost creativity. She claimed it healed a lot of her anxieties and self-doubt. She said one day we'd go picking for mushrooms and she'd show me what it's all about, although I'd previously heard that it's quite similar to acid, yet the intensity differs depending on the dose, and so do the visuals. Either way, I was more than eager, especially because we seemed to understand each other, and I had the feeling we'd bond on a spiritual plane. There were conversations between us that were yet to be spoken, but I knew they'd be good ones—so, I endeavoured to spend more time with her and explore them.

Over the next week or two, we began holding hands everywhere we went, not in love, or with the intent for it to lead to anything romantic—possibly because my brain was still infatuated with Fritz—but it was more the comfort we found in each other. It sounds childish to look so deep into something as molecular as the basic action of holding hands, but for me, it's always been a rather intimate connection. Eyes, touch and smile: those three factors are important when it comes to being intoxicated by another human being.

Regarding the situation on Fritz, I'd never heard of this after-effect with MDMA—I even ran a few searches in case other users had experienced the same phenomenon—but it seems my mind had repeated the drug-influenced view I had of Fritz over and over, which made me feel like I couldn't connect to the highest degree with Zoe, until one fateful night.

*

On a Tuesday evening, about three weeks into our Sydney stay, I heard a banging—initially, it sounded like somebody was frustratingly trying to shut a stubborn drawer that just wouldn't close. During this obnoxious drum beat, I was smoking some weak pot in my bedroom alone. Cannabis didn't count as a 'one-time' drug on our previously stated list. As an in-betweener, it quenched the thirst for trying new things as our listed substances weren't so easy to come by. I began walking through the hallway to investigate the noise, thinking I may have smoked a little more than expected. By the time I reached Fritz's bedroom, I was about to warn her that there may be the danger of a massive, ferocious rat rummaging throughout the apartment or some other ravenous rodent to keep an eye out for. *Maybe those animals are bigger here*, I thought. Usually, Johnny was the man to call in these situations—he'd heroically stomp or exterminate the damn thing without blinking. I always had the jitters when it came to crawlies.

I knocked on Fritz's door and I must've mistaken her "Don't come in!" for "Please, come on in, pal!"

As I opened the door, I saw Fritz in bed with Johnny, both naked, exhausted and sweating profusely. High, *what was I supposed to do?* I couldn't act outraged—she didn't even know I had these strange feelings for her, and I couldn't at all blame Johnny. He just happened to make a natural move on her. I closed the door awkwardly without speaking a single syllable. I got into bed, feeling quite shitty and I realised that it was probably exactly what I needed to disconnect myself from the idea of Fritz. Johnny got to her first, and now, it was possible to set forth with Zoe. It stung, for sure, but it seems it was a blessing in disguise. The only problem was, I didn't have a lot of time to spend with Zoe as we had already booked a two-week stay in the Gold Coast before setting off to where we eventually agreed to visit—*Thailand.*

We had only two days left to spend in Sydney.

*

The night before leaving the Harbour City, Zoe invited me over to her apartment to try this new strain of weed she acquired from a friend a few months prior. Everybody we knew there lived in some kind of apartment; they were more city-like folk than Johnny and I ever were.

Zoe's apartment was small, but it still had this cosiness about it. A pinkish vibe with pastel purple undertones as if it were plucked out of some late Wes Anderson film. *Genuineness and decadence entwined.* I wondered if she invited me over to solidify our relationship in a private setting but unlike Fritz, she never gave off that aura. Zoe was more of a mystery and she always kept those feelings to herself. I initially made a conscious plan to see where it went and hoped that maybe I could land a kiss or something more, so as to justify the amount of time we were spending together—but truthfully, there was one thing I hadn't counted on.

We kicked our feet up on her balcony together after a few drinks as she took one of two joints she'd been saving out of a ziplock bag. As soon as the bag opened, my nose hairs felt as if they were seared. *This was some strong shit.*

"A joint each?" I gestured to the remaining one in the bag.

She only laughed at the expense of my naive comment. "More like a puff each. This stuff is vigorous, Clark." She raised an eyebrow, handing me the pre-rolled joint as she retrieved a torch lighter from her bag. "Go *easy*. That's a warning. This is probably gonna be the strongest dope you've ever tried. I've been saving them for a special occasion."

I've had my ins and outs with cannabis, so I didn't quite heed her warning as instructed, especially with my ego bubbling higher with every new substance I was trying. At this point, I may as well have considered weed to be in the same category as cigarettes. Zoe took a couple of puffs and handed the joint over to me. I expected a cakewalk, especially after getting partially stoned in Fritz's apartment the week prior.

I inhaled deeply, and as the smoke entered my lungs, I accidentally swallowed and coughed like a hundred-year-old chain-smoker. "That was strong," I croaked with squinted eyes.

Zoe cackled. She took one more puff and called it a night, "Jeez, I'm stoned already."

I hadn't felt a thing yet, wondering if maybe my tolerance stood in the way. Zoe sat there for a short while, in between cackling and telling a story. By that time, I reached my ninth puff with no notable changes. I wondered if it was *ever* going to hit me, until I rested my head back on the seat. *Shit,* I thought. *I can't lift my damn head.* Zoe was laughing louder. Surely, she was aware of my tremendous struggle. With great effort and a skull that weighed twenty kilos, I lifted my head and looked at her in an attempt to seem unaffected.

"Tell me about your tattoos," I slurred in a higher-pitched voice than expected. It felt as if I were listening to myself on record.

"You all right, darling?" She smiled. I noticed her eyes blinking rapidly, as if she were trying to hydrate the redness around her pupils. "I was in the middle of telling you the story about Fritz and the lesbian cop"—she held herself from giggling—"then I looked over and you were gazing at Saturn's rings."

I just stared at her, trying to get a word out but my mouth didn't want to move. This was comparable to a drawn-out, dampened *nang*. I was in trouble, and this bud seemed to hit me like a point-blank sawed-off shotgun. I suddenly found myself stuck in this cycle where Zoe would tell me a story and I'd obnoxiously laugh at literally anything and find myself, *and* her, stuck in a phase of repeated laugher, toppling sideways, then once again, telling a completely different story and cracking up mid-sentence again into this same loop of limitless laughter. It was frightening because nothing was funny and there were no feelings of happiness or joy, just pure laughter for no reason at all.

This was not your everyday marijuana.

I tried to speak, realising that only when I spoke could I think or perform actions with conviction. The only way to feel normal was to continue talking or focus on completing the task at hand, like adjusting my seating position—but the second I stopped or took a breath I was yet again halted in a complete daze, unable to move or speak. *Ineptness.* The basic rule was to keep moving, or remain frozen. I found myself forcing out words to maintain functionality—well, as functional as you could be in a state like this.

"Every time I ..." I couldn't get the words out. And each word exited in a different octave, sounding completely goofy. I tried my best to explain the phenomenon to her, but I continued to lose track of my thoughts because I kept pausing. "Every time I speak, I have to keep ..."

At this point, I knew we needed to get inside, or I'd end up greening out on the balcony. Plus, I was overly thirsty to the point where water was the only thing on my mind. This was quickly turning into a regrettable trip. I managed to get off the seat and walk inside to retrieve a glass—I must've taken at least ten minutes. I downed a glass and promised Zoe a full one, so I poured another and placed the cold bottle of water in the fridge before grabbing the glass to give it to Zoe. *It was empty.* I was in a state of confusion: either I imagined pouring her a glass, or I just drank *her* water. After finally bringing her a full glass of water, we returned to the lounge room.

After a sudden feeling of nausea and throwing up, most likely caused by the alcohol before smoking or swallowing that first inhale, I expected to be in for a shitty night of exhausting recovery, but I was stopped by Zoe in her pyjamas.

"I've got a bed set up for you across the hall. You sure you're all right?" She handed me a full glass of water. Her state of mind and motor skills were far more advanced at this point.

"Thanks. I'm feeling fucking horrible. I'm just gonna try and sleep this off."

"Have you ever listened to music while high?" Zoe

looked deep into my eyes. I was swaying at this point, dizzy, yearning for a pillow to rest my weary head upon.

"Nope." I shook my head. "I've never been this fucked-up on green before."

"Listen to a bunch of your favourite songs." I was hoping she'd finish her sentence quick because I couldn't balance myself there much longer. "*Trust me.* You'll thank me in the morning." Zoe kissed me on the cheek and smiled.

God, what a gorgeous smile. Even with dazed eyes and messy hair, she was something to behold. I trusted her word, and did as she instructed, knowing I massively underestimated an overly strong strain of weed, and that I needed something just to ride out the rest of the experience.

Music on drugs. *Holy fucking shit.* As I rested in bed, I felt the vibrations run through my thighs. Tingles and nerves rushed down my body with every beat, every kick drum and every melody that each song threw at me. My body was part of the music and it felt as if those nerves shocking my thighs were in synchronisation with the sounds I was hearing. Upon closing my eyes, the experience heightened. Patterns, merging and combining with each other, almost comparable to when you rub your eyes vigorously and visualise faint patterns, except I had no control over these and they seemed to swirl, chop and change by themselves according to the music I was listening to—which was alternative indie rock at the time: *The Strokes*, to be specific. As every song had its own story and new strands of thoughts and realisations attached to each one, I noticed new chords and background riffs in the music that I'd never discovered or even considered before. It was like hearing the song again, but how it's supposed to be heard, and from a new perspective, which caused my love for this music to grow heavier and mean so much more to me.

Then, not long before I fell asleep, I had an epiphany. My thoughts focused solely on Zoe and my sudden love and gratitude for her and the time she was spending with me, even though she didn't need to. I lay there in bed for at least an hour, watching time fly by but then slow down to almost a complete stop at times. I smiled so much; I could've cried. The only worries I had were my fleeting thoughts, having such great realisations and ideas about myself and who I am, but by the time the next introspective thought pattern appeared, I'd completely forgotten the last.

Zoe saved my experience. She flipped it one-eighty from nauseated uselessness to an enlightening melodic journey. This trip was something I wouldn't forget any time soon. It went from my worst experience with marijuana to my best in a mere few hours. One part of me wishes I spent more time that night sober or on a subtle high with Zoe, but another part of me was thankful for having this experience altogether, even if the best part was spent alone.

*

Listening to music on Fritz's balcony with a coffee and a cigarette overlooking the railways—although I'd never been much of a smoker—Zoe and I discussed what my next plan of action was with Johnny, who I think at the time was still scoring in the bedroom behind us. Zoe turned up the radio, playing a song by *Paramore.*

"I hope you don't think of me as some *drug-crazed* psycho-bitch." She exhaled. "I'm a careful user and I only pursue substances that benefit me. I see them as tools—especially the natural side of things."

"You've never had an addiction?" I queried. "I mean, with everything you've tried, you haven't had the yearning to return to the good stuff?"

"I don't think I have an addictive personality. I've never abused a substance." She shook her head and began tying her hair up. "And most of the drugs I seek out aren't actually addictive. Especially natural psychedelics. In fact, the more you use them, the less desirable they are."

Zoe had a high respect for drugs and rightfully so, especially the ones that can benefit our state of consciousness and explore our perceptions of the world and our very existence. She had a small box she was willing to pass on to me, having already experienced everything inside that box. Contained within was a small block of cocaine, about half a fingernail worth—*which was more than plenty.* Some dried shrooms, which I promised I'd take with her and *her* only. Deeper in that box, she possessed a few more MDMA caps and a small bottle of liquid mescaline—a direct extract from the succulent, thanks to some home brewing.

May 19th

While packing my suitcases with Johnny on the closing day of our Sydney stay, I showed him the box and he riffled through it.

"Zoe said we can have whatever we want. I just feel bad—I don't want her to think we're using her." I sighed. "I really like her. I don't wanna give her that impression."

"Take it all," Johnny said abruptly, shutting his suitcase.

I shook my head. "Did you listen at all to what I said? I don't wanna take advantage of Zoe. It's not nice."

"Is she gonna use it?" Johnny shrugged.

"No."

Johnny snatched the box, shoving it into my suitcase.

"You and I are very different." I began zipping it up.

He looked at me, serious. "What's that supposed to mean?"

"Nothing, Johnny."

Leaving Sydney, there was only one thing I didn't want to leave behind, and that was Zoe. However, Johnny and I had an agenda, and we weren't even halfway through. We took the entire box with us and were soon on our way.

We set off to the Gold Coast. I wish I told Zoe more of how I felt—I didn't even get to kiss her. Johnny didn't care about Fritz one bit—they seemed to be strictly physical. I wondered if maybe I should have admitted that Zoe meant more to me, that maybe it would've planted the seed to reunite with her in the near future.

Chapter 6

SATURDAY NIGHT AT THE CONTINENTAL

Polydrug use can either enhance or reduce the effects of a drug, depending on the substances, the dosage, the chemical reactions, set and setting. We yet again had to drive to our next destination only because we weren't able to take the flight and go through customs with the overwhelming amount of contraband we had on board.

"How pure's the coke?" Johnny asked, watching over the beaches alongside the road and dipping his fist into a bag of sweet chilli chips.

"It's literally a piece." I chuckled. "A solid rock. Zoe said she's got a good connection."

"Well, I'm most excited to give that a taste. What *you* should've tasted though, was Zoe." Johnny shook his head in disappointment as if I'd missed an opportunity to shag.

"Dude, she's not remotely the type of girl I'd sleep with and forget. In fact, *I'm* not that kind of person at all."

I tapped my fingers on the steering wheel. "You should know that. I'm not like you."

Johnny kicked his feet up on the dash, shoving a handful of chips down the chute. "Should've at least kissed 'er."

He wasn't wrong. I regretted not making some kind of move. Most of our road trip consisted of me pondering these thoughts in silence, letting them swell incessantly inside my brain.

The choice was either Brisbane, or its unruly cousin, the Gold Coast. The Gold Coast seemed to be the fun, more bustling town, but what really solidified our decision was Johnny's cousins. He had three boys there who invited us to stay with them. Not only would they provide potential connections to other substances on that list, but lighting up the town with other people made these experiences fresher and distant from the earlier ones. On top of that, a place to stay meant we could save some funds for the real travelling.

At first, Johnny got along with his cousins a lot more than I did. They were somewhere between Middle Eastern and Turkish descent and seemed to have an array of pre-established inside jokes that I hadn't been privy to.

In the kitchen of the townhouse, Yarim, the eldest cousin, who was about twenty-six, was lighting some coconut shisha charcoal on the stove while Hassan, a year younger and a little skinnier, was texting some girl he'd just met.

"Bro, bro. Tell her to come to Alambra, cuz. We're all gonna be there Saturday. She can bring her biddies; we'll all get lit," Yarim yelled from the kitchen while Hassan typed frantically on his phone. *As if that was a line any quarter-brained female would consider.*

"Nahhh, man. Play it cool," clapped Johnny. "Show her you're busy, bro. Never beg a chick to come out. Send her a pic of you at the club and she'll feel like she's missing out."

Johnny seemed to become a different person around these fellas. In fact, he managed to change his goddamned accent to suit the Middle East more so than he did before. And his usual persona was known to steer *well* clear of that stereotype.

"Oi, shut the fuck up—let me type," squeaked Hassan. "She already saw that I read the message, cuz."

"So, what's in the box, bro?" asked Mehmet, the youngest, fattest of them all.

When asked questions like this, I immediately felt I was about to be jumped if I hadn't given up the information requested—even though Mehmet was barely sixteen, it felt as if he were speaking for the three of them.

Hassan smirked. "There're no Snickers bars in there, Mem."

Johnny and Yarim cracked up. I turned to Johnny, and he nodded with a shrug. "It's coke off the rock," I said. The faces of all three cousins lit up like Christmas at the Super Bowl.

Yarim nudged Johnny's shoulder. "Fuckkkk, bro! I knew you'd finally pay me back for that hot hook-up I got you on New Year's."

Yarim placed the coal onto the shisha and Mehmet took the first hit. He then strutted over to me and threw his arm around my shoulder. "This *cunt.* This cunt right here is a fucken baller."

I think he expected me to laugh or think it was some kind of patronising praise. I simply nodded and decided to replenish a few brain cells by finding my bedroom alone, which happened to be beneath the stairs on a fold-out army cot. I listened to the boys in the kitchen as I fluffed my pillow.

"Bro, send her a pic." Yarim continued to razz Hassan. "She's got massive tits. You have no choice."

This was going to be a long stay.

*

The guys wanted to go out for a night on the town, but I was far too wrecked from the drive and told Johnny to tag along with them. I told him I wanted to kick my feet up with a glass of wine and a short novel. Truthfully, I wasn't so comfortable with these new acquaintances and wanted a couple more days to get to know them before trusting their antics on a night out.

I was sitting in the kitchen with *The Simpsons* playing on TV, texting Zoe and learning about some stalker guy who'd been blowing up her phone for a week straight, insisting that she send photos of her feet ... which we both found insatiably hilarious, and more so when I told her to instead send him a photo of mine. Meanwhile, Johnny's cousins were playing ping pong with booming psytrance music in the basement. Johnny trotted upstairs to grab a few cans of whisky and coke.

"Comin' down, or what?" Johnny nudged on his way past. I noticed him glance at my backpack on the table and knew *exactly* what his next question would be, regardless of my response.

"Man, I'm just tired tonight and those guys are bit overhyped. I appreciate them but I don't feel like getting into ping pong right now." I leaned back, hoping he wouldn't ask.

"Chuck me that coke, will ya?" And there it was, as casual as ever—he'd probably rehearsed it three times on the way up the stairs. Johnny wanted Zoe's coke to share with his snorty friends who'd probably finish the whole baggie within the hour, especially if they tried to compete with who could shoot the most lines. As a whole, their temperament was far too predictable.

I shook my head, "It's Zoe's coke—"

"Yeah, but she gave it to *us*," Johnny interrupted, desperate. "Be cool, there's fuckin' heaps. You can't possibly shoot that whole rock yourself." I had the feeling he'd already promised it to his cousins that night, boasting over its purity.

"She gave it to *me*, Johnny. I'm not gonna share it with these guys I just met. They're gonna abuse the bag and leave us with nothing. It's expensive shit, too," I replied. Johnny shrugged and shook his head. He clearly didn't want to let his coke-craving cousins down.

"They're literally giving us a place to stay, bro. We should appreciate them a little more. Besides, you didn't even pay for it." Johnny tried the old manipulative approach, but I wasn't buying in. In fact, it was the first time he'd called me *bro*, which meant, for sure, he was becoming his cousins.

I knew that as soon as he returned to the basement with the absence of coke, he'd paint me as the villain: *the guy who's squatting in their house and withholding the snow gear.* I knew he'd blame me for his false promise and further divide me from the rest of them. It just didn't feel right to give away what Zoe had given to me. I was happy to share, or even give the whole bag away—but not before I'd tried it and done what I told Zoe I'd intended to do. I'm sure she wouldn't have been too happy if she heard I'd tossed the bag to a bunch of airheads in a basement without trying it myself.

Cocaine is easily one of the most notorious drugs known to man, whether it's earned that crown or not—so much that I probably needn't mention it. Most people rack lines to feel like a Columbian drug lord because it's 'cool' to say you shot twenty-one lines in a weekend. I've always been sceptical of it and whether it lives up to the hype of being such an infamous compound. Most of the time it's snorted or rubbed on your gums and sometimes it's smoked or even injected. While on the matter of intravenous administration, Johnny and I made a pact never to go as far as injecting a drug—it was the only other rule we created amid this monumental journey that probably should have had many other rules considering the risk and dangers involved in the royal sport of drug-fiending.

Nicknames are, again, numerous: C, Coke, Nose Candy, Snow, Angel Dust, Star Dust, Charlie—the list goes on and on. It's also one of the only drugs that they can't test you for, especially since your body breaks it down quickly after consumption, which makes it near impossible to trace. Coke is made from coca leaves mostly down in South America. To extract the pure, white cocaine, they use household products such as cement powder, battery acid and bleach to separate the liquid from the solid. I've always wondered why cocaine had been so villainised, but after learning how it's made, I realised it was more of a personal health risk than anything—not the high you receive from it, especially when cut with something like talcum powder, lidocaine or simply *sugar*. Keep in mind, these nasty buggers shouldn't be entering your lungs in the form of *anything*.

*

A few days in, Johnny had already been out a couple times and I decided if I wasn't going to have the opportunity to go with Johnny alone, I may as well tag along with those godawful cousins of his. It was a Saturday and usually the biggest night of the week to get out and I told them I was tagging along and was willing to share the coke. Yarim rolled up a twenty and shot the first line after dramatically acting like his mind was blown over how pure this coke looked. Next, Hassan took the second line and passed the note to Johnny who—to everybody's surprise—shot it up quicker than you could see the line disappear. That simple action earned him the nickname The Human Vacuum—as you could probably tell, creativity was running at a peak high.

At this point, I knew it was coming to my turn. Mehmet shot it up in theatrical fashion as if he were Tony Montana on the brink of death, before passing the rolled note on to me.

Yarim nudged Mehmet. "Bro, it's not sugar. Relax, Tubby."

The boys giggled and leant their heads backward to help the powder sink in. *This is it.* I pushed my left nostril shut and leaned in close. On the way in, Johnny mentioned to keep the note just above the plate surface for a clean shot and I realised it went up much easier than I'd expected. I could feel the bitterness enter my nose before sniffing heavily to get it all sucked in. After leaning my head back and opening my eyes, the cousins were already shooting their second lines. Johnny fucked up his second one and had to frustratingly line it up again.

"Don't make me revoke that nickname, Johnno!" Yarim chuckled.

Next, we decided to play ping pong after skolling a few drinks and getting back onto our feet. I decided to pace myself with the one line and see how it felt. I noticed the boys getting hyped up and excited. I decided to shoot another to get on the level, feeling like it hadn't hit me yet. As I sat down for a second line, I felt this bitter, bitter taste in the back of my mouth from my nose—they call this *the drip*. I had a sip of booze to wash it down before snorting the extra thick white line. At that point, my front two teeth became entirely numb. I couldn't feel them at all, but it was a satisfying sensation, nevertheless.

"Yeah, I'm starting to feel the Bugs Bunny teeth." I'd spontaneously come up with that name to describe the sensation and it seemed to be a hilarious statement from the perspective of the cousins.

"Bugs Bunny teeth?" Hassan pointed. "That's a mad name for it, cuz! I'm gonna use that from now on."

After about four minutes, my adrenaline and nerves shifted into hyperdrive. My limbs wanted to move as the others began nodding their heads to the music in the background. I demanded a ping pong bat and played doubles alongside Johnny. My blood pumped and when standing still, I could only move on the spot, striking the bat continuously on the table to match the musical tempo and clapping intensely to expel the overwhelming amount of energy I'd been charged with. *Holy fuck.* I just wanted to smile, clench my teeth and stomp on the spot. The frequency in the room had changed, and we were *all* on it.

"Now he's feeling it!" Yarim pointed at me and stuck his tongue out.

Suddenly I felt like one of them, hyped and in sync, matching their energy.

"I knew this cunt had it in 'im." Hassan slapped his hand on the table.

Is this how these guys felt most of the time? It's a feeling where you want to be a complete dickhead and have a fun time doing so. It's the first time my anxiety seemed to disappear in seconds, and I felt part of the group, finally matching the beat of their overstimulated drum.

"Try this, bro," danced Mehmet, handing me a glass of what looked like diluted orange juice.

"What's in it?" I asked. We always need to be cautious of these things, especially when mixing substances.

Yarim pointed to my backpack and thanked me for sharing my vodka with them, although I had no vodka in that bag, and they were too drunk to realise that it wasn't Russian water in that bottle ... but Zoe's liquid mescaline.

"Oh fuck," I said to myself before yanking Johnny aside. "Did you drink that drink?" I asked extremely quickly, not only over the rising concern but the coke made my heart beat three times the usual pace. It felt *good*, it felt *right*. It felt as if thousands of volts of expendable electricity had been charging and weaving rapidly through my every vein.

Johnny laughed and shrugged. He was also fooled into believing it had been vodka in his cup. "I just thought that sour taste was the Queensland oranges!" He'd downed a quarter of his glass already.

These guys had already drunk so much, and their tongues and teeth were so numb that they weren't even considering if they'd been tasting vodka or something completely different. They were about to trip way over their heads. Unfortunately for them, it's adequate karma for rummaging through a backpack that isn't theirs. But this also meant a major dose of something they'd probably never ingested ... mixed with a wild stimulant, hard alcohol and an unsuspecting brain—the recipe for a catastrophic disaster.

Johnny gestured with rage. "Shit. Shit, shit, shit!"

"You'll be all right, just let the coke wear off and sit down for a bit," I reassured him. While stationary, I could feel my ankles still matching the pace of the song, as if the nerves in my legs had minds of their own.

Johnny's face was rife with concern. I could see the beads of sweat forming on his forehead. "About an hour ago, the boys and I shared some Dexies."

I looked at Johnny. "How many?"

He shrugged. "Two to three."

"*Each?*" I raised an eyebrow.

Johnny nodded, almost shaking at the thought of some kind of overdose or psychotic episode. Dexies are a pill form of Dextroamphetamine meant only for the treatment of ADHD, but like Ritalin, many teenagers use it to give them an energetic buzz, especially if they aren't diagnosed with the disorder. But that wasn't what Johnny and I were worried about. At least *he* had a solid head on his shoulders and knew the doses of what he was dealing with. The oblivious and unpredictable *cousins* were the problem.

We were left with a choice: either ditch the bastards and let them figure it out all by themselves in the basement (which may be considered a safe setting for something unexpected like this) or drag them out to the club and see what happens.

"Let's tell them." I sighed.

"What? No," Johnny snapped. "They'll lose their shit. They'll get defensive and paranoid."

I knew it wasn't right to allow someone to unknowingly trip their minds. "If we don't tell them, they won't know what the fuck is going on. In the worst case, they could *kill* each other."

We decided to do the right thing and tell them about the mescaline that had been very wrongly mistaken for vodka—*it wasn't even the same colour*. It was only fair to inform them of what they'd just ingested and what to expect—even though I hadn't tried any of the stuff myself.

First came denial.

"You're fucking with us!" Yarim was shaking, pointing at me, hoping I'd crack up in laughter, but I was as straight as a one-dollar bill. "It's fucking vodka, bro."

Next came fear.

"Holy shit, *holy shit!* I've never even tripped before, cuz. What's gonna happen to me?" Mehmet clutched his head, inadvertently putting himself in a bad headspace which didn't help the mescaline that was already coursing through his youthful veins. "I'm gonna overdose! I'm gonna fucking overdose!" Maybe it wasn't such a good idea to tell them.

Then came anger.

"Why the fuck didn't you label it? Are you a fucking retard?" Hassan gestured across the room as if I'd done it on purpose. As if I'd slipped it into their drinks for my own twisted amusement.

And finally, came acceptance.

"So, are we going out or not?" Hassan asked. I don't know why, or how it got to that point, but even after they'd passed all those stages of concern, their stubborn attitude of expecting a wild night seemed to prevail. This was happening, and I wasn't stopping them.

I decided to turn them loose at this club called The Continental. *For sure*, I thought, *the effects would probably kick in after we entered the club*. Since Johnny was already dosed up—just not as much as them—I decided to taste a bit for myself, just not enough to get the bum's rush. Especially when dosing on two or more drugs, safety *always* comes first.

As we stepped into the club, it had already been booming. Johnny raised his eyebrow, gesturing me to look down at his pocket. He'd brought the remaining coke. He winked at me before concealing it in his jeans.

"We go to the bathrooms for when we need a bump," Johnny said. "I told the boys we're fresh out. So, the rest is ours."

The issue with coke is, as soon as it fades off, the comedown hits hard and you're immediately sluggish which makes you feel the need for another sniff. When you're on a coke high, you can almost drink as much as you want without getting sick or too wasted. It completely erases any nausea or disorientation. But when peyote is added to the mix, things may get a little wild. It made me wonder if it'd help me stay sober during a trip, and maybe even assist in navigating the trip, controlling it as if I were lucid. After dosing a bottle cap of mescaline—compared to a *shot* that the others took—I was prepared for the effects. My feet stepped along with the music as if I were in perfect sync with the percussion. I looked over to Johnny's cousins, who'd already been in two scuffles so far in the night, just not enough to be kicked out for—they were dancing like those wavy, inflatable tube men you see at the car dealerships. I decided to float around to different people and chat with them, knowing these guys were probably going to be thrown out on the street sooner or later and I didn't want to be tripping peyote when that happened or get caught up in the middle of it.

I spent the next fifteen or so minutes getting to know who I'd been in this melodical place with—coke makes you more talkative. For some reason, the people seem to be a lot nicer and laid-back in Queensland.

Among the music, we could barely hear each other speak. "I'm Natalie." Short and brunette with beady eyes, she held out her hand. *Painted black nails.*

I shook it and kissed her on the cheek for some reason. I don't know why. It felt right. "I'm Clark! I'm a little high at the moment."

Natalie giggled. "Where are you from, Clark? Your pupils are *really* dilated." Her voice muffled against the music. I tried desperately to hear, only making sense of the sentence with her gestures and the few words I could make out.

"I'm from Melbourne." I turned to search for some kind of mirror to inspect the dilation but there was nothing of the sort unless I went to the bathrooms. "Where are you from?"

"Dalby. Here in Queensland." She smiled, moving her hips to the music, syncing with the drums and the rhythm. "I work on a farm and I'm only in town for a week."

We spoke for at least another fifteen minutes, but I can't seem to remember what else she said before the mescaline kicked in at full swing. We were on the topic of music and at this point, she had her arms around my neck.

"I've always loved the *Pixies*. I've been to three of their concerts." Natalie's voice began to wobble as if she'd been trembling. Her voice fluctuated, heightening in volume before lowering to the point that her lips were moving with a lack of words. This wasn't even the height of it.

"Ding's about about fifffffty years old now now now-now-*nowowowowwww*." *Fuck*. Her voice was doubling up on itself, and her words were no longer matching her lip movements.

I could only nod to show her I was listening, hoping she didn't think I was bored or losing focus. I didn't want to come off as rude. Upon nodding, my vision began shaking as if my lens had come loose, layering and overlapping. Surely, by this time, Natalie knew I'd tuned out on whatever story she was telling because she seemed to have disappeared.

Now, this was the interesting part. The colours of the club began changing and vibrating with the music. The walls expanded in and out as if the room were breathing and we were inside the lungs of the venue. I could feel my body swaying with the hot, breathing air. I sipped water to see if I could calm it down—not to stop the trip, but in hopes it would slow me down, so I could prolong the experience and enjoy more of the night rather than black out. I turned around, looking for Johnny's cousins but they were nowhere to be seen, and neither was Johnny. At this point, I could no longer take in the music. It was all just a big blur of audio, and the visuals only became more intense and vibrant. If this was the power of mescaline in a bottle cap, I wonder what a 50 ml shot would've done to those cousins of Johnny's.

I found Natalie again and she was laughing hysterically. I wondered if she'd been laughing at me, at the fool I made of myself. I soon noticed that I could only see her eyes, closed in front of mine. I wondered if the mescaline was causing my vision to employ some kind of zooming effect, but I quickly realised that she was kissing me. I couldn't even feel it. Her wobbly face in front of mine and her tongue, likely in my mouth. I don't even know if I could have pouted or positioned my lips at the time, but she seemed to be doing all the work. She then grabbed my hand and smiled at me. Her smile halted my action as I stared at her for a few seconds, mesmerised in awe by her beauty, or at least the endless space of planetary stars within the pupils of her eyes.

When you look into someone's eyes on mescaline, it's the most intriguing, hypnotic thing you could feel or ever understand. It was like a million spiralling galaxies resided within—*infinite space*. I tried not to give her the impression that I was staring, so I focused on other parts of her face as she tried to speak to me amongst the music. I wasn't even going to begin to try and decrypt her words. I was too far gone. Her facial muscles stood out, moving and overlapping. I remember wondering why I hadn't noticed all these movements in a human being's face before. Each twitch, each muscle, each molecule working together to convey expression. It made her emotions far more demonstrative and comprehendible. I could almost read her mind as she spoke, seeing her soul and what it wanted to say. I couldn't only understand what she was saying, but what she *felt*—even though I couldn't hear or understand her language. It was as if we weren't even speaking English anymore, just simply understanding each other on another plane of communication—almost like how we'd picture aliens to interact with each other. We were feeling it together even though she wasn't on the drug. Natalie was special, but she wasn't the only one. Everybody I saw was special, beautiful, both significant and insignificant at the same time. We were all meant to be there, in that place and in that moment.

Natalie walked me through the crowd. It didn't take a genius to guess that we were headed to the bathrooms. Although, when we got there, there'd been some kind of incident. About four security guards were blocking the bathrooms and I tried to catch a glimpse behind them, but the guards—and the mescaline—hadn't allowed me to see past them. I turned to Natalie, and she was gone. Either I spent too much time around the guards, trying to get a glimpse, or she realised I was much higher than she thought, and ditched. I even wondered if I'd imagined our kiss, but I was sure that I hadn't been *that* far gone. I then noticed three boys screaming and kicking their legs, being dragged out of the bathroom by security. Yes, it was exactly who I expected—Johnny's cousins. I couldn't hear their voices well, but I could make out what they would've been saying from the sheer expressions on their faces.

Yarim, pulling away from the security guard with wide eyes. "Help me! He's trying to kill me!"

Hassan was speaking in tongues, or at least, that's what I could make out, "Youda-fucken-ramsing-fleshningg!" His teeth were clenching, his lips bleeding, as if he was desperately trying to stop his face from tearing apart.

Mehmet was the last to be pulled out, except he wasn't speaking. He was allowing the guards to escort him out while he cried to the ceiling with tears running down his face. One could only imagine what these poor souls had been subjected to.

Whacked out of their brains, it made them look a little like junkies. I knew this would happen, but I wondered where Johnny was in all this mess. By about 2 a.m., I found myself sitting down, watching the club go by in fast motion—I could guess I'd been sitting there for just over an hour but in this state of mind, it's difficult to keep track of the existence of time. I thought I was coming down, satisfied with the nature of this wonderful drug and the euphoria it gifted me. I was dead wrong—it wasn't over. Suddenly my legs began floating beneath me. As these people danced in this club, my body rose to the ceiling— that had been violently rippling in an infinite pattern for some time now. I wiped my eyes, and I was fifteen years old.

Now, this may not make so much sense, but these are the kinds of trips I'd been on the search for. I just never expected something like this so soon in the journey. Fifteen years old, at school, trying to compliment this girl, Amelia. I complimented her beautiful eyes, constantly, thinking that each time I said it, it could spark some kind of breakthrough—*a childish approach.* A thought process began—the strategy was flawed. She smiled and nodded at my compliments, flattered but nothing more. That was as far as I could ever get. She'd heard it all before and looking back, mature and adult, I was never supposed to compliment her; at least, not to that extent of persistence.

Within this vision of the past, I began to believe that showing interest in a crush in front of her would trigger some kind of chain reaction to get her to like me. It was all so real, yet so surreal. I could see the scuff on her nose ring, the chip in one of her painted fingernails. The imperfections in her teeth at close proximity. I wondered if this was as far as the mescaline would take me—yet it wasn't. My brain warped me through a lifetime of being with this woman if I had a better approach of gaining her attraction, from dating, to arguing at a movie theatre, to getting married, to having children—two daughters—and sending them to school. From getting divorced, to getting back together, dealing with one of my daughter's struggles with finances and relationship abuse, all the way to sitting on a porch with my wife when we were old and grey, flicking through photos of our lives and holding hands. At this point in our old age, she wasn't Amelia anymore—she was myself, looking right back at me.

I woke up in a daze, on the street. I'd been thrown out after passing out in the nightclub. I began breathing fast as the mescaline seemed to have mostly worn off. I didn't move. I sat there for about a half hour, registering what the fuck my brain just put me through, about how a single change of attitude towards a human being could've changed the entire course of my life, whether it was for better or worse. My brain latched on to this idea that I'd unlocked another timeline, an alternate universe for which my life would've been different, before I'd even lived it. That universe was real, living—I was just not in it. I shook my head, trying to brush away the thought. I'd previously been told not to take these experiences too seriously. I could easily lose my mind over the contents of this trip—and some people are known to have—but you can decide to learn something instead. That everything we do—every single expression or word we say, or action we take—can change everything, for the rest of our lives. I wasn't going to contemplate anymore. It was as simple as that. I'd constructed my own advice that was going to stick with me for the rest of my life.

Chapter 7

WHEN GOD LIGHTS HIS CIGARETTE, THE WHOLE WORLD GOES UP IN FLAMES

I won't lie, I thought about it for days after, maybe weeks. It's impossible to go through something like this without it festering in your brain for at least a little while. The upside is, it wasn't about Amelia—I could really care less where she was at the time. Of course I was curious, but not nearly enough to contact her. It spoke to me as if our spiritual bodies were connected in some way, as if we'd already lived that life together and we were back to being younger, trailing down different routes. But this wasn't about her—and I was glad about that. I never wanted to regret anything in my life. That dream only provided me with the realisation to understand how important a single movement, a single word, a single touch or a blink of an eye could impact the course of the rest of your life. The almighty butterfly effect. *Was what I dreamt completely fabricated over something I may have desired a long time ago? Or was it a vision into another life?* It could've been something that represented some alternate universe of some kind. What troubled me was seeing myself looking back at me. My own piercing eyes glaring at the origin from which they came. It was haunting, and I interpreted it as the fear of being left alone with yourself and your thoughts until death—and how horrifically confronting that must be. Although, I could've been completely wrong and misanalysed this information. The dream seemed to be communicating to me that I shouldn't squander any opportunities, or I could be left in regret. Mescaline is a very powerful and profound substance from the peyote cactus, originating from the use of indigenous tribes in Northern Mexico for communicating with God and the spirits for power, guidance and healing. Drugs like these are to be highly respected. *Peyote is no party drug.*

*

I woke up at Johnny's cousins' house with a headache and a nosebleed. I hadn't noticed the bleeding until I saw the residue on the pillows. My stomach was flooded with alcohol. I hadn't realised exactly how much I consumed because the cocaine had been masking it, fooling my drunk mind into thinking it was somewhat sober. After showering, I noticed Johnny on the balcony with a coffee, listening to music. His cousins were all in bed. I assume they were burnt out after their horrific experience at the club. As much as I wasn't their biggest fan, I didn't want anything dangerous to happen to them, and I'm thankful it didn't. The most I heard was that they hurried to the bathroom that night and were tripping so hard that they remained in the cubicle together, eventually attacking each other and being forcibly removed from the bathrooms for creating a dangerous space for the guests— which was the part that I witnessed. This goes to show that a *bad* experience on a substance won't necessarily mean the drug is to blame—but the fact that it was abused by the portions of consumption.

As I stepped onto the balcony, the acidic aroma of coffee almost made me gag.

"Where'd *you* disappear to last night?" I confronted Johnny having not seen him since he was dancing at the club. "You get kicked out, too?"

"Boy, you must've had a cracker of a night." Johnny laughed, sipping his brew with his feet up, unaffected from the night before.

"What do you mean?" I shrugged. "How come you look fine, and I'm all fucked up?"

"I never went to the club, man. You were adamant on going and my cousins were already on their way out." He shook his head at me. "You got amnesia, or what?"

I didn't believe it. I saw him at the club. I even *spoke* to him. Maybe it wasn't him. I was sure of it, though. He hadn't even come out with us. I remembered him leaving the house with us. I was even sure he had the rest of the coke bag, until I noticed it was in the pocket of my own jeans.

"Completely calming and soothing," Johnny claimed after I asked about his personal peyote trip experience. "I threw up in the bathroom first, but then I came out, took a seat and closed my eyes. These colours, Clark. These fucking *colours*. I can't explain them because they don't exist. Try to explain colour to a colour blind person— that's what it's like." He stared in awe off the balcony into the distance. "I saw an outside portrait of myself and who I am. I appreciate everything—or at least, want to try to from now on."

As I listened, I had never heard Johnny speak so philosophically before. It's like the mescaline unshackled a new perspective with unconceived thoughts that provoked his very beliefs. Fortunately for him, he'd been in a safe place with little disturbance and a moderately safe amount of mescaline to trip on his own.

June 4th

4 missed calls from Zoe
7 unread texts from Zoe

Zoe was in town, and coincidentally with perfect timing. I couldn't understand why she'd come. Maybe she felt we had unfinished business. I needed to see her, and somehow tell her how I felt, considering the awakening trip I just encountered. It was as if the peyote passed on this message to me, then sent me this specific person that I may have wasted an opportunity with: *Take it, take it before you miss it completely!* This could've been one of those things, that if I didn't take action or make the right move, I'd be stuck with a lifetime of wondering 'What if?'. And how could it be, that I'd been in town for nearly two weeks, and she'd decided to show up the *morning* after a trip of realisation? It was all too coincidental not to mean anything.

As I walked with Zoe on a day trip through one of Queensland's rainforests, I explained my thought-provoking trip. I knew she'd been through these experiences before and could potentially dissect it from an outside perspective.

"Mescaline can do wonderful things. It was a good mixture, that one," she said as we walked through Lamington National Park. The smell of nature was damp with crisp moisture in the air, somewhat more appreciated in a time like this, and in the presence of somebody I now held dear.

"I had a vision of my father once." Zoe's voice slowed and she took a breath. "He spoke to me during a trip on peyote. He died not long before I was born but his voice was so real, so true to what I imagined and heard in old videos." She pursed her lips, looking to the sky as she walked ahead of me. "It was a shitty time in my life. I was anorexic, and on the brink of depression and used psychedelics to escape. Not abusing them or mistreating them but it was a sense of euphoric liberation for me and from my social life."

"What did your father say?" I asked, trying not to cross any lines of comfort. "Did you speak to him?"

She nodded, looking away from me. I assumed it was a tear she'd been holding in. "He told me everything was going to be okay, and he loves me and he's sorry he left me." Zoe turned and hugged me. I caressed her as she continued. "I never believed anybody who's ever told me that until he did. Telling somebody that it's going to be *all right* is usually interpreted as a figure of speech, but from him, he meant it, and it meant everything to me. It was real."

I held Zoe for about a minute in my arms. I closed my eyes, inhaling her familiar scent from the few weeks before, and realising I'd grown accustomed to her presence and felt somewhat cold without her.

"I've never told anybody this before. Not even Fritz. Not even my mum, who'd probably want to hear it more than anybody," she admitted with her head in my chest. "I don't know how she'd take it. How do I explain something like this to her, and how I came across it by utilising a drug? She'd say it's ridiculous and completely disregard it—not to mention her disappointment in me."

"Most people are uneducated and ignorant." I said, running my fingers through her silky hair. "They put heroin and meth in the same category as reefer and shrooms because they're all classified as *drugs*. I don't blame your mum for being conditioned against them. Most people are."

I don't think I've ever been so close to a female. Sure, I've had a few girlfriends, slept with a few women and had lasting relationships but when you connect with someone on a spiritual plane, it's another feeling entirely. I trusted her immediately.

"So, who's Amelia?" Zoe asked, biting her lips with a smile.

I laughed to myself. "*Somebody* sounds jealous."

She playfully slapped my shoulder. "Seriously. I wanna know. She must've been important if she was the sole focus of your trip."

I sighed, even though basking in the limelight of jealousy felt momentarily desirable. "A simple crush from when I was younger. I can't believe my brain pulled it out of nowhere," I admitted, hoping she wasn't thinking it was the *girl* that I'd been obsessing over, "It was the principle of the trip, the meaning behind it. The example could've been about anybody. Even you."

Zoe giggled, covering her mouth as she blushed and playfully punched my shoulder.

As we continued our trek through the forest, she opened up about further experiences with psychedelics and how she even had a boyfriend she'd done acid with and by the end of the trip, they had the same experience about a scorpion's life and how it was a living, breathing animal like us, considering it to be more than just a predator that yearns to kill, but an animal that is simply striving to survive. What blew her mind was, there were never any prior thoughts, conversations or pictures—or anything remotely related to scorpions—when they had this parallel experience.

"It had me believing that two minds can be connected, bound." She looked at me in deep thought. "Maybe that's evidence that the universe is telepathically interconnected somehow. I know it sounds stupid but I had a friend that tried shrooms for the first time, and he told me that as he consumed the substance, and as the psilocin heated his body, he felt as if the mushroom actually revealed the secrets of its life to him, and the fact that it's an organism, wilfully passing information onto him for education and better understanding of what life *actually* is."

Zoe was an introspective being. Most of what was going on in her life was in her mind, travelling, learning, reasoning and wondering—eternally wondering about who we are, why we're here, the divine powers and tools to assist us in discovering these things further.

"You're a honeybird," Zoe claimed as we ventured through the trees and reached a river.

I laughed, unfamiliar with the term. "Is that some kind of insult? Should I be offended? Does honeybird mean I'm some kind of coward?" It was just like me to assume the worst.

She shook her head with a grin. "You're curious, even when you know nothing of what you're curious about. You're happy to throw yourself into the beehive for the honey, accepting the potential stings that come with it." She looked at me and squeezed my hand.

Zoe considered herself something of a honeybird. She later explained that honeybirds often expect one outcome—a kind of hypothesis—but come out the other side with a more educated understanding of what they were initially looking for, rendering their original objective to be completely irrelevant.

After a few hours, Zoe and I came across an old factory in the distance. It looked like a nuclear power plant with cooling towers, yet it couldn't be because there are no reactors in Australia, except one in New South Wales, and even that one isn't made for electricity or to produce power, it's only for medical and scientific purposes. This reminded me of nuclear power and the fact that there are substances, chemicals, rules and physics in this world that can't be fully grasped or explained, and probably never will be. This was a reminder to keep an open mind and wonder about my own inner being and what I can learn about myself through these 'tools' Zoe had mentioned. Maybe I *was* becoming a honeybird.

I decided that before we set off to Thailand in two days, I had to make a move and listen to what my trip had passed on to me.

"Come to Thailand with us." I held her hand, pleading with her. "Johnny won't mind."

"Now, you're asking too much." Zoe laughed and shook her head. "I have a job back home and I'm not even free until September."

I simply couldn't change her mind, and Johnny and I weren't stopping here, especially with my current state of self-discovery—it would be far too soon to quit.

I kissed her. This time I felt it. Our lips came together, and I could feel the embrace and yearning meet me within her supple lips. She was a lost soul, and so was I. This occurrence even made me rethink my journey, wondering if I should've stayed in Australia, just for her. I couldn't do that to the cause, and I couldn't do it to Johnny. I wasn't quitting the journey before leaving the country, or without pushing it as far as it could go.

Chapter 8

DISSOCIATION AND CONFRONTATION

Waking up in a bar in Thailand, I dreamt about her again. Zoe's smile, her eyes looking into mine, holding both my hands in a field of green. After these drug experiences, I seemed to dream more vividly and remember my dreams with clarity. It only raised more questions. *Was it a mistake to come here? Had I just turned down a moment that the mescaline trip most urgently told me not to turn down?* I looked to my left at a few girls staring my way, extra skinny and typical Thai. I turned to my right and noticed Johnny dancing on stage with a few girls of his own. He was having the time of his life as they shook their fake boobs in his face. He laughed. These shows are never really supposed to turn people like us on. In their culture, they may find it arousing but for people like us, coming from overseas, performances like these were more amusing and cause for embarrassment than anything. Johnny later told me that one of the dancers grabbed his hand and placed it on her breast to tantalise him, but he described it as being as solid as a rock, and that he's never felt tits that hard in his life. Obviously being fake, and likely not even being female. It was Thailand, and over there, you had to keep your guard up—the catcalls and groping that women are subject to in Australia, men were equally treated this way over in Thailand, and it was refreshing to see them have a taste of their own hostile tendencies.

I had drunk a little too many Long Island ice teas on Royal City Avenue, the biggest street for nightlife in the country. Crowds everywhere, music booming out of nightclubs and spilling out onto the streets, merging with the guests of other dance clubs. This was a partying country, and what better place to try some new substances? Johnny had already slept with three women by this point, and we were only about a week and a half in. It would've been four if he hadn't brought one of the Thai girls home to later find out it was a Thai *boy* when his clothes were removed ... Not in a hundred years would I be letting him live it down. The only way to be truly safe when sleeping around in this country is to hook up with other travellers like you, that are there for similar reasons to yours.

Approaching me at the bar, Johnny nudged my elbow with a smile. He wanted my spirits as high as his, and he ordered a few more from the bartender.

"I don't know why I like it." He licked his finger after taking a shot of cheap Scotch. "Maybe it's a good comfort."

"What, the shenanigans on stage?" I smirked.

He shook his head. "The meaningless sex. It's good—

really good, don't get me wrong. I can get most women I meet into bed within the evening. It's honestly easy when you know how to talk to them and show them what they wanna see in a man."

I raised my eyebrow, wondering how much more his egotesticals would swell, waiting for a *but*.

"I woo them, act for an hour or so like we're in a relationship—as if they're the summer special and get them into bed. Forgotten before the sun comes up." Johnny slid the next shot away from him, declining it. "But connection is the problem. The physical aspect is tip-top as a vanilla drop. I just don't know how to find that spark that tells me that it's real."

I looked away from Johnny. The more time you spend with someone, the more travelling you do with them, the more conversations you have with them—you tend to realise who they really are and the true thoughts trailing through their minds. *The brain behind the mask.* This whole time I'd been somewhat envious of Johnny's sex life and how exceedingly active it had always been. I was never one to kiss and forget; in fact, I seem to get attached to things too easily, and above that, I never possessed the kind of confidence he boasted. *Everybody has one superpower.* Johnny could charm nearly every female he'd come across, getting them infatuatedly wrapped around his finger in seconds. As for *my* superpower, I possess the talent to hold my bladder for extended periods of time ... not quite as compelling, but indubitably effective when lacking nearby restrooms.

I was wrong about Johnny. He was a human after all, and did, in fact, desire genuine emotion—something far deeper than what he'd been accustomed to.

"Well, Johnny." I patted his shoulder. "The grass is always greener on the other side, my hairy friend. I *wish* I had your confidence; I *wish* I could share a connection with a female that lasts more than three seconds and *not* catch feelings."

We downed a few Cosmo shots before stumbling back to the hostel.

June 25th

There was a while where I felt too attached to Zoe, and it would hinder my excitement of going out and getting shit-faced because my mindset would be in the wrong place. I'd end up having a regrettable night. Johnny came up with plan while drowning himself in aftershave at the window overlooking the city at 10 p.m.

"Tonight, we're switching personas." He nodded with confidence. "I'm gonna attempt to get to know somebody and actually connect with another human being. Spark up a real conversation without it ending in sex."

He turned to me as I threw on a new knitted white shirt that I picked up at the market that morning, which for some reason, my nipples insisted on poking through.

"And you"—Johnny pointed at me—"are gonna get into bed with somebody tonight. I assure you. With a wingman like me, you cannot fail, *Squire*."

I smirked at his optimism, at the fact that he thought some kind of meaningless hook-up ought to mend my ailing heart. The night simply didn't end up that way.

Every night in Thailand is a party night, and I set out with Johnny, two boys and a girl from the hostel we were staying in. One of the boys had a baggie of ketamine pills that he sold at the nightclubs every evening. The group called it *Phuketamine*, although we were nowhere near Phuket. Compared to Australia, the laws in Thailand are far less restrictive. For Johnny and I, that meant the drugs were far easier to come by, but a *lot* more hazardous. As concerning as it is, ketamine just happened to be on our list. Judging from how strange and peculiar this place was, I don't think it mattered how fucked up we got. It was also probably the first real risk we'd be taking during this journey. Weed and alcohol are moderately safe, MDMA is relatively safe from the right people and if not a heavy dose—the same goes for cocaine and mescaline. But ketamine in another country from a stranger means anything could be in that pill—*anything.* Jacob was our guy and he'd make from $250 to $700 in a single night by selling this shit because in this country—local or tourist— cheap drugs are a specialty, and besides, *everybody wants to get fucked up.* The only reason we trusted the bastard was because we shared the same hostel—and if the product was bad, he'd have myself and a raging Johnny to answer to.

Ketamine's a form of anaesthesia but it's used as a dissociative—the effects of the consciousness detached from the body or its environment. Before this experience, I'd only spoken to a friend who tried it once before and he described his legs as quivering like jelly and a loss of control in the movement of his limbs while on the drug, especially as the trip progressed. This experience happened inside a Melbourne club, but my expected experience would be inside a Thailand rave—a similar, but very, very different setting—and possibly a different kind of ketamine, considering the origin. Again, I didn't know too much about it at the time. Ketamine's considered one of the safest substances in terms of predictability, but that doesn't mean a heroic dose is safe—or any dose at all. I remind you; drugs aren't something to take lightly. They can be monstrous, vicious and deadly with many factors that can completely diminish you and your ego as a mere human being.

The nicknames: Special K, KitKat, Horse Tranquilizer and Ketters. These names aren't quite as creative as the slangs of its predecessors, but the drug itself wasn't even supposed to be a drug. It's a sedative used for pain relief in humans and animals, but recreational abuse allows for the user to feel disconnected from reality, sometimes to the point of reaching hallucinations under heroic doses. For us, this sounded intriguing, so we thought, *why not*? You may be thinking that I'd just contradicted myself by saying *don't take drugs lightly* but this is a matter of my experience at the time and a reflection of my age and level of maturity retrospectively.

*

Popping the ketamine in pill form, I knew it'd take a little while longer to sink in. We hit this club where you had free entry on the condition that you buy a drink—*a ridiculously expensive one*, although four bucks of ours was like gold to them, so really, it wasn't *quite* as wallet-squeezing as it sounded. I was anxious, waiting for it to kick off. I wanted the night to launch for real, but I wasn't about to consider taking more—we'd already learnt our lesson from the LSD about two months back. At 11:30 p.m., Johnny had been talking for quite a while to this short, drunk girl and I grew impatient with him, wondering why it was taking so damn long for him to return to me. Maybe he was following through with his intentions of getting to know someone. I thought it'd be easy for him considering the vast array of women he'd already had in his hostel bed—which by this point probably had more broken springs than that of a five-star whorehouse. Maybe she was playing hard to get. Maybe he was playing with his food. I was getting irritable and sweaty in the crowd amongst the body odour and bad breath, so I strutted over to him with my ginormous drink, comical bucket hat and shades that barely fit my head. As I veered closer, I noticed that she wasn't much his type— pretty, no doubt, just not Johnny's usual swing in the old batting cage. Aside from that, she was notably distressed. Johnny turned to me as I approached.

"Dude, we gotta help Kimberly," he muttered into my ear, quickly looking around as if the tax man was on her ass—or the border patrol. I had trouble hearing him which is common when I'm drunk in a large crowd. "We can't leave her alone."

I shrugged, glancing into her eyes for signs of pupil dilation. "What, is she overdosing?"

He shook his head and continued scanning the entire club. It was then clear that a predator was on the loose. I looked around too, not knowing what gender, or what in the hell I was looking for. She could've been running from a fruit bat for all I knew.

"We gotta get her outta here." Johnny's lips were on my ear. "This guy offered to help her out 'cause she missed her flight, and she stayed last night at his. And now he's stalking her. She reckons he slipped her something but whatever it was, it's yet to take hold."

I knew we came to Thailand for fun, I knew we came to Thailand to document its drugs. But I didn't know—I couldn't have known in a million years—*that we'd be superheroes*.

She was shaken, clearly frightened out of her wits. "He's a little funny-looking. He has a moustache. I think he's French or something." Her eyes were pale as if she hadn't slept for days and she had to place her drink down to avoid spillage from all the excessive nervous twitching.

At first, I expected the usual hook-for-a-hand, scar-on-the-face, eye-patch story but describing him as French made me, by default, picture a man in a striped sweater and a beret, holding a baguette and relentlessly terrorising the Thai nightlife. *Sacre bleu!*

After showing a photo of the perp to Johnny, he laughed. "Kinda looks like Steve Buscemi." I cracked up but Kimberly wasn't so amused—either she didn't know who Steve Buscemi was, or she more likely wasn't impressed by our humorous outlook at the time.

"He was really nice, like *really* nice to me. I forgot my passport in the apartment and missed my plane, so he offered me a bed to sleep in." She was on the verge of tears having to explain it to the only people who'd listen. "At first, he didn't pressure me or harass me. I just thought he was a good person."

After all, that's how most of these situations ignite. I came up with a simple solution. "Let's just get her outta here to another club, or she could even stay at our place. We have a girl in our hostel and a spare room. It's gotta be safer than there."

Unfortunately, that wasn't the issue. Kimberly shook her head and bit her lip. Her voice was now squeaky, like that of a yawning fox. "He has all my stuff in his apartment. My passport, my phone, my wallet and keys." The temperament of her voice was clearly due to her anxiety, which was quickly bordering on panic.

This didn't sound like something that would be rectified with ease—especially when awaiting a horse tranquiliser high. I looked over at Johnny, wondering how far he was willing to take this, considering the imminent decline in our abilities as we attempted to aid this poor girl. One minute, she'd be talking to a courageous, attractive man willing to save her from the dragon's dungeon—next minute, she'd be talking to a slurring Scotsman with a withering consciousness and floppy limbs. Johnny gave me *the look*, which meant he wasn't letting this go until this girl's property had been safely reclaimed, no matter how fucked up we were, no matter what she came down with, no matter who got in the way—that was a quality I valued in my companion, Johnny. I must admit, I did wonder if Johnny had ulterior motives—some kind of payment for helping her out or the typical offer for her to stay in his bed after the ordeal was done and dusted—but Johnny deserved a little more credit than that. He was simply a good person which is difficult to come by these days. It was time to get this girl her belongings, and maybe knock some sense into a pig with a moustache.

We walked her through the club and out the door as she told us exactly what he did in detail. First, she woke up with him lying beside her. Second, he crafted her a sandwich and was adamant that she eat it, as if she were starving and her life depended on it—so, she did for some reason.

"I knew it was time to go because he was getting weird," Kimberly explained. "But then he wouldn't open the door unless I promised to sleep with him."

After hearing this, I leaned over to Johnny in whispers. "She seems too young to understand the fundamentals of travelling abroad and the lines between *safe*, and *sketchy as fuck*."

Johnny nodded with a raised eyebrow. "My exact thoughts."

However, it didn't matter who was at fault or how she found herself in this mess. What mattered, was how we were going to get her out of it. Somebody up there must not like her very much, because somehow, she ended up at the club to find a couple of ketted-up males to help her out.

On the way through town, we even ran into a few of our hostel mates, repeating the story to them and having them tag along as if armed with pitchforks and torches. Kimberly received a message to meet at the 7-Eleven a few blocks down the street. With now eight of us in a group, we were able to track down this lunatic swine to get him to unlock his apartment and allow Kimberly to grab her shit.

My worry wasn't getting Kimberly home safe—I already knew this would happen considering our dedication to the cause and how hell-bent we were on teaching this dumbass a lesson. My real worry was when the fuck this lacklustre ketamine was going to set in. I even closed my eyes, wondering if I was feeling it yet, trying to forcibly kick it in and hoping for some closed-eye visuals or *anything* to set this chemical into active flow, but it hadn't caught on. I was only kidding myself. Before taking ketamine, we'd also heard about the possibility of falling into a *k-hole* which could be similar to a closed-eye psychedelic trip and the mind-blowing exploration of your consciousness. But this was only under heavier doses of the drug, although you can never really count it out, depending on your body size, how much you've eaten, the dose potency and about a million other factors. A k-hole would be a welcomed, journalistic experience for me—just not in a place like this, or a scenario like so.

We reached the 7-Eleven where Justin—Kimberly's predator—was holed up inside. Truthfully, I expected his name to be something along the lines of Pierre, or Jacques. At this point I noticed Kimberly holding hands with Johnny. From his perspective, she was scared and required security, but I worried that Kimberly was too inclined to trust strangers which was probably what got her into this mess. Justin was even more rat-like than the pictures. I wondered if this was a frequent scenario for him and maybe even some kind of routine that was backfiring. He chomped into a Mars Bar and noticed Kimberly outside with now *ten* people behind her. He fumbled the chocolate in dramatic fashion and picked up a payphone inside the store, pretending to make some kind of call as we waited outside.

"Don't go in yet." I halted the group.

"He's right there," Johnny opposed. "We could take him down, now!"

I stood in front of Johnny. "We can't go in. It'll look like some kind of gang robbery." Kimberly gave me this sour look as if I were trying to protect the bastard. "The cops are gonna see us as a bunch of teenagers causing havoc. We don't want the cops involved, dude." I then mouthed the word *ketamine* to Johnny and he realised it was the right call to avoid the law.

I wasn't sure how cool I'd be if the police held us up as the high was peaking. Johnny and I waved at Justin, but he pretended not to see us. The store manager noticed us outside and looked over at Justin—he must've thought he was one of us, performing a suspicious deed inside. He quickly shooed Justin out, forcing the phone to hang on its line—it was time for the confrontation.

Kimberly seemed quiet all of a sudden. With her passion in the story she told, we assumed she'd go ape shit and beat him up herself with the backup she had. It made me wonder if she *did* lead him on at all, or give him any false impressions, and that maybe he simply got a little too attached. My guess is, she was only telling us half the story. Nevertheless, we crowded him as he threw his hoodie over his head, rushing down the street as we walked quickly beside him like the raving paparazzi on a common celebrity. We hadn't thrown a punch—it simply wasn't our style to go in guns blazing. We just wanted to get Kimberly her stuff back. Although, I shall admit that this team exercise was getting quite fun and exhilarating. Chasing after this creep was almost recreational.

"Where's your apartment, bro?" Johnny yelled in his ear, intimidating him with so much as an arm's width to breathe.

I nudged Justin's shoulder. "Give the girl her stuff back. Don't make this difficult."

Agent Burrows, FBI at your service.

Some random girl who happened to tag along with us decided to take it a step further. "Rapist!"

Justin turned and punched me, right in the teeth. *What the fuck just happened?* I wasn't expecting to be struck. I found myself on the ground in a blur. I looked around and all these voices were loud, hazy, intense and screaming. Above me, I could see a bunch of hands fighting with each other. I assumed Justin was attacking the others, or they'd all jumped on him after he lay the first hand. I tried to get up, but my vision was miles from where I thought it was and my head felt like a stack of three bricks that my body tried to helplessly balance. The ketamine had taken hold, and it was one strong motherfucker of a pill. My legs wouldn't move to get up—they'd only wobble back and forth like I'd fallen into a bowl of thick raspberry jelly.

"Get ouuuuuuf me! Staaa oupp!" is apparently along the lines of what I said, or at least *tried* to say, according to the guy helping me off the ground.

Being pulled onto my feet, I lost balance, holding myself up against a brick wall. Kevin, this super-fat guy who looked like a naive, gullible character that'd be the first to die in some eighties horror flick, straightened me up.

"Dude, are you all right?" Kevin held my arm in case I was to make passionate love to the ground again. "I didn't think he hit you *that* hard."

I noticed the mob moving down the street as Justin seemed to flee during the distraction. My brain felt absent from my head while Kevin was talking to me. I could understand him but I couldn't speak anything more than what I'd already attempted. It was as if Justin knocked my consciousness out of my brain and onto the street. I felt myself nodding at Kevin while hanging onto a wall for dear life, as if it were an impossible task. For a second, I wondered if I was dying and some Thai demon had been waiting to possess my body after my soul had risen out of it, but then I realised—*this was some kick-ass ket.*

"We gotta get to Kimberly," I slurred.

Kevin navigated me back to the group, crowding an apartment building—I knew it was Justin's apartment as the mob seemed to be waiting for something. The only sensation I really felt was the elephant weight of Kevin's right foot trampling on my own feet—aside from that, my body was almost floating in thin air, painless. I began to like it, realising I was supposed to feel this way. When you're having a trip of any kind, stressing or fearing it only makes it worse, especially when you don't know what to expect. Now, when you embrace it, even when it's unfamiliar territory, you begin to like it, immersing yourself in the journey, whatever it may be. This is one way to pull a one-eighty on a seemingly bad trip, whether you just ride it out and endure it, or turn it into something incredible.

As I reached the crowd, I noticed somebody crouched on the ground. Somebody else had fallen. At first, I thought Justin went Super Saiyan, taking on ten ninjas at once like Zatoichi. I then realised it was Johnny on the asphalt, scraping himself off the ground and cackling at the sudden high he'd gotten from the pill.

"Ha *haaaaa* what da fuck?" I felt slightly embarrassed for him but no matter because the mob was focused on the task at hand.

It hit him hard. I wondered why it took so long to kick in and came on so strong. I concluded that it was either cut with something and the effects didn't act as they should have—or, when I was knocked to the ground, the sudden rush of blood and adrenaline forced the ketamine to rapidly spread through my system, hitting me like a swinging mallet on a merry-go-round.

Kimberly entered the apartment with Claudia and Matthew—two recent additions to the mob—to retrieve her stuff. It was only right that Johnny and I were to go in with her and put an end to this madness but considering our disabled capabilities, we were in no shape to go inside. Kimberly exited with a bag of her stuff, ignoring Justin as he quickly closed the door to get us the hell out of his face. On the other side of the ratty screen door, the mob yelled and cursed at Justin, throwing half-eaten apples and empty fruit smoothie cups in his direction.

"Get a life!" yelled a voice I couldn't quite make out,

followed by another: "Leave the young girls alone!"

He could've simply shut the heavier door and been done with it, but he tried desperately to rescue what had remained of his dignity.

"She came onto *me!* I didn't rape her," he pleaded as if on trial.

Claudia yelled in her American accent, "Go inside and jerk off, asshole."

Justin continued. "I *helped* her! She should be thanking *me*. You only heard one side of the story."

As Justin continued ranting and raving with all his might, we'd lost interest and decided to head back to the hostel to let Kimberly set up her room and sort her belongings. She even threw out all of her socks and underwear, in the case he'd fiddled with them or tampered with anything—a good call.

Thailand's interesting, and a lot of men (and women ... and ladyboys) are only there for quick pickups and cheap sex. It's a prime destination for crazy, horny, thrill-seeking druggos to get blasted and satisfied together with a touch of alcoholism and ping pong shows to make the whole spectacle complete. I wondered if we should've stayed there longer but it was Johnny's turn to pick the next location, and he was excited for our next stop: *Europe.*

Chapter 9

LOOK OUT! SALLY D'S GOT A GUN AND SHE'S GONNA BLOW YOUR FUCKING BRAINS OUT!

Mark my words. I never wanted this journey to get dangerous. If I were writing for sport, maybe it would have been a safer adventure. But who knows? Let's say, theoretically, I was called to Amsterdam to journalise a sporting event like football. I could simply die in a plane crash, or a car accident, or slip on the street and hit my head on some fire hydrant. *Dead.* This journey happened to be based on substances that enter and affect our bodies and brain chemistry. If we were supposed to die, we'd have our numbers called. Whether the subject is drugs, sport or simply writing an article about the effects of global warming. I know it may seem ignorant or naive, but we were never out here in search of danger.

Johnny booked us this fashionable place in Amsterdam. He was never honest about how much he spent and every time I asked, he'd hit me with, "Don't worry abouuut it," in a comical Jersey accent.

The apartment had these purple walls, but they weren't tacky or cheap, it was somewhat wealthy and elegant with a multitude of gold-painted ornaments and sculptures—clearly themed for a picturesque stay, although Johnny and I viewed it in a different light.

"Not a bad place for a trip." He rubbed his hands together in anticipation.

One of the many good things about Europe is that the booze is dirt stinkin' cheap, and so are the cigarettes. "My liver and my lungs are gonna hate me after this," I said, looking up at the menu in a local bar and seeing full mixed cocktails costing less than three euros.

An alcoholic's heaven. Johnny and I were in line to capitalise. He purchased eight cartons of Marlboro cigarettes upon arrival, and I lugged six bottles to the apartment. Two whiskies, two gins, one rum and a Jägermeister. Our apartment was set up for a rowdy party, but no event of the sort was to be had, and no guests were to be entertained. Amsterdam was the first place on our trip where we hadn't had roommates or friends to stay with. For a little bit, it seemed like we could get into less trouble that way—but after a while, we realised it was cause for concern. When you don't have friends around, you tend to go looking for them—whether it's in the right places, or the wrong.

"Arrghaahahah *hahaaaaaa* ..." Johnny was already cracking up, making friends and hearing the life stories of locals at a pub called De Tulp. The neon signs beamed over the jungle-themed setting inside the venue.

"This lad is hilarious," Eoin, an eccentric Irishman, tall, lanky and bald, called out to one of his friends who'd just entered. "He's Australian, ya know?" he said in his rough accent.

"Unfortunately." Johnny clinked pints with them, splashing Guinness onto the floor.

Johnny always had a talent for effortlessly making friends with new people whether they seemed his kind or not—somehow, he'd naturally find something in common with them and he'd make a temporary best bud. This was a technique I could never understand or perform myself. I would work so hard to the depths of my brain to think of something I could talk about to connect with a stranger, but it'd only result in a blank. Then, my brain would simply start obsessing and focusing on the fact that I couldn't think of something—further hindering my chances of a decent conversation. I guess it was simply a talent Johnny possessed, or a matter of self-confidence.

Eoin laughed and gestured to the both of us. "So, what are yous in town for? Surely not the *beer-drinkin'* contest? You Crackerjacks'll lose." He sniggered.

"As intriguing as that sounds, we're actually on a bit of a journey." Johnny smiled. He then looked at me, knowing we'd have to explain what the hell we were doing this far from home.

"Well, fuck *me* in the butthole," said Eoin with his hands on his hips. "This is some mad shit you're into, fellas. Listen close—Somersby Lane," he said, writing an address down on a napkin. "That's not the street name.

This is." He handed the napkin over. "If you're on a drug-fuelled journey and you want somethin' fresh—try this joint out. It won't disappoint."

*

The first couple of days in Europe were spent wisely—smoking down as much legal marijuana as we could get our hands on. The green stuff isn't only stronger there, but it doesn't smell like pungent dog shit either. Let me just add that it's very, very pure and clean shit. When something's recreationally legalised—which is almost anything in Amsterdam—it's refined and cultivated to perfection. Which is a pro in terms of legalisation for other countries hoping to achieve the same. This means more access to the product, higher-grade substance, decreased lacing of hazardous chemicals and a higher chance of actually ditching an addiction because it's so abundant that it doesn't need to be sought out, smuggled or be considered such a precious, scarce substance to obtain. And for the record, whoever claims that you can't possibly be addicted or develop a constant psychological dependence on weed—*you're in denial, pal.*

After a few days, we were already bored with smoking up two days in a row and felt that the need for weed was hitting a brick wall—as mellowing as the high was. But we were ready to place the joint down and move on to knocking off some of the listed substances. Unfortunately, we hadn't actually been able to cross any off the list in Holland—*believe it or not.* But there were some substances in Amsterdam that *hadn't* been on the list, for better or worse.

August 10th

It was a Thursday evening and we'd had a few drinks in us already. I made sure to stop once we were feeling tipsy enough to slur a sentence or three. Reason being, if we were to try any new substances, we didn't want the alcohol to either ruin the high or negatively interact with it, especially not to throw up or feel nauseated—that's a hefty buzzkill when you're out on an evening of promise.

We arrived at Somersby Lane, where Eoin directed us, to this tribal-looking man with a huge moustache in a quiet little laneway. He looked like some performer welcoming us into a circus—although there was no circus at all. In fact, it seemed a little ominous—but surely, we thought, our new pal Eoin wouldn't lead us astray.

Drunk, Johnny shrugged. *"Why not?"*

Under the influence, you're usually persuaded with ease, tempted by things much quicker and allowing the night to swing like a pendulum in any direction it so chooses. Johnny grabbed my hand as we walked towards this small door in a dark alley with flashing lights. I then realised that maybe I had a few too many gin and limes back at the apartment.

"Do I look normal?" I tugged at Johnny's elbow, gesturing to my face. "They might not let me in, dude."

Johnny raised his eyebrow. "Pfft, does this look like a place that's gonna give two shits?"

This place definitely wasn't the usual Saturday night rave we'd been expecting. However, it was a welcomed adventure. Upon entering, the beaming red neon lights on the walls and dense atmosphere made us feel like we were quite heavily intoxicated—more than we already were.

Johnny shielded his eyes from the bright neon in the dark room, making it difficult for his eyes to adjust to the exposure. "If I was tipsy before, I now feel like an all-out Irish soldier on his day off."

The jazzy tunes sent muffled bass vibrations through the walls and through my veins as if it were a whole new sensation of intoxication. It felt like we were in the decorated bowels of a living creature. Warm, musky and the smell of fog machine fluid.

As we found a free booth, it was as if the other guests were preparing for some kind of show. I assumed a strip show because usually these things were down dark alleys in dark clubs with shadows and neon throughout. The flashing lights out front were a sure sign. Johnny licked his lips in anticipation. I noticed nearly everybody in every booth pull out a joint and a lighter. I soon realised that this was the perfect atmosphere to smoke up. Two guys occupied the stage, a massive dude with a classic bass and a much shorter, stumpier one playing a jazzy electric guitar at a slow pace. It wasn't a strip joint after all—*sorry, fellas.* Cigarettes have been banned indoors from 2008; however, there are certain bars like this one that allowed pure joints, no tobacco or anything else. But some don't always play by the rules. Soon enough, a tall, inconspicuous woman—as gorgeous as she was—approached our table with her Austrian accent. Bright red lipstick was her defining feature.

"Sage twenty-five ex?" She smiled with her purse opened. We couldn't make heads or tails of these words.

"Is she hookin' us up with prostitutes?" Johnny whispered in my ear.

I smiled at her, whispering back to Johnny, "Kinda sounds like it, doesn't it?"

I then noticed a bundle of joints in her purse. *It must be some kind of cannabis strain*, I thought, which was of course welcomed. And if she had nicknames for them, it was bound to be some intriguing shit.

I shrugged, thinking of the only possible thing I could say. "Why the fuck not?"

She smiled at me before digging through her purse, pulling out a very regular-looking joint and passing it to me. It cost me twenty euros which was quite expensive compared to the rest of the pot we'd been burning in the nights prior. She offered Johnny but he shook his head, reluctant to spend the money but also having a little surprise of his own. As the woman hovered to other tables like a seahorse through a reef, a glass pipe appeared discreetly from Johnny's jacket. He'd smuggled it in.

"What the hell is that?" I asked, partly offended that he'd keep something like this from me.

Johnny sighed and leaned over. "Tina," he whispered with a cheeky grin.

It turned out that Johnny acquired the pipe earlier that day and was waiting on an opportunity to smoke it with something he'd called 'special'.

"If I'd told you about this earlier, you would've been against it." Johnny sniggered as he pulled out a lighter.

I wondered what drug I could possibly be against in a situation like this but after he inhaled, I soon understood what he meant by keeping it from me. Johnny inhaled his pipe with a heavy intake. His aim was always to get in as much as you can, because to him, there's nothing worse than an underwhelming dose of anything. Almost immediately, he sat back and stared at the ceiling as if out of breath with a smile. He turned to me, holding back an excited giggle.

"Holy fucking *shit*." Johnny's neck was bobbing, and his legs were restlessly stomping with excitement. A tonne of radical nerves resided within.

Ice. Crystal Meth, Glass, Rock, Frosty, Shard ... Tina. Johnny had just smoked ice and was ready to paint the town transparent. As excited as Johnny was, crystal meth is likely the most dangerous drug in history. It's addictive, *heavily fucking addictive*. It's much easier to overdose. It's cut with bullshit nearly no matter where it's from, and when you get hooked on it—it's near impossible to quit, suppressing your hunger to make you lose extreme amounts of weight at a rapid rate. For some users, you don't try anything after trying ice. Either the ice is the hook and there's no attraction or yearning for anything else, or ... you're dead by the time you think about it. I decided to steer clear of it for now.

"Let's give sage a swing," I said, taking a deep breath with little to no expectation—a strategy to avoid disappointment.

I kept an eye out on the inconspicuous woman who reminded me at the time of Cruella De Vil. I wanted to make sure she stayed around because if the product is bad, the dealers tend to split quickly to avoid confrontation— but she remained in plain sight. I even had second thoughts, but Johnny's peer pressure prevailed.

"What've we got to lose? You might not get a chance to try this strain again."

I knew it was simply part of the experience. It's normal to question these things. Interestingly, it didn't smell anything like weed. I lit the joint and breathed in, sucking the air into my lungs and letting it sit there for a little, anticipating some kind of unexpected high. It tasted different, woodier and more minty. Blood was normal. Breathing was normal. A few more puffs went by. *Bloody hell.* Leaves began growing on the walls. *Fuck.* I felt as if I were strapped into the seat of a rocket ship, bracing for imminent lift-off. *Holy shit.*

My nerves disappeared, I felt needles in my chest; the atoms that made up my body shrunk and warped until I was sucked into some kind of shoebox and my entire body was condensed—compressed to the size of matter at a molecular level. Then I knew for sure, this wasn't weed—not at all.

I heard Johnny speak. "Breathe, breathe, breathe-breathe-brea-bree-*breeeeeeee*—"

I could no longer see. My vision was wiped clean and all I could hear was Johnny telling me to breathe repeatedly. At the time, I wondered that maybe in the conscious world, I'd forgotten to breathe but at the same time I'd forgotten *how* to breathe, feeling panicked and stressed over whether I was literally suffocating myself to death. I hadn't had the time, nor the capability to process a question and ask myself what this mysterious substance was. My mind felt stretched beyond its full capacity—not a single thought was comprehensible. *I could feel my brain pulling itself apart.*

Within all this madness and staring into nothingness, I saw slight glimmers of green. Leaves. Leaves all around me, swaying, growing and breathing in unison. Relief washed over me. I didn't need lungs. I was the tree itself, taking in the carbon dioxide and releasing the oxygen back into the world. Each branch was a limb, and each leaf was my gift back to nature, as if I'd grown the leaves for the world to admire and take benefit from. I sat there planted for two thousand seven hundred years. I watched humanity go by, day by day, feeling every second and every minute of every day, every hundred years watching the world change and morph around me, from rivers, to tribes, to farms, to villages, to ancient cities, slowly growing and evolving. I experienced an immense feeling of gratitude from the world surrounding me, as if smoking whatever I'd smoked was thanking me for it, showing me another world as a gift. At that point, I'd actually forgotten how I got there, or what substance I'd taken to feel this way. A whole new plane, a whole new dimension. The idea of physical existence or actually considering the physical realm from which I came was far beyond comprehension. In this world, the physical realm didn't exist. There was an overwhelming presence of a woman, but I have no words to describe it—whether she was in sight, in spirit, part of me or showing me all this— it was comforting. I believed I'd be here forever, as if my organic body on Earth had died and I was living on without it. I felt acceptance, as if it were all going to be okay. Life continued to grow around the tree that I'd become until even modern times had passed and the collapse of civilisation followed. Buildings in ruin, the death of humanity, the smoke-filled skies and as the year 2700 had struck with a great magnitude of destruction—at that exact second of turnover into a new year—I was overwhelmed by this heart-breaking emotion, wasted, exploited, exhausted in despair. I glanced down at my brittle branches, and my leaves were burnt and decayed. *We humans have destroyed the world.*

My eyes opened and I was lying down on the booth seat, staring up at the ceiling, and noticed Johnny holding my shoulders and looking down at me, asking if I was all right, although that's only what I assumed he said. Truthfully, I couldn't understand him. I could only describe it as blurred words. According to Johnny, I was also speaking in tongues. I assumed that my literacy was in perfect order.

"Ourrrrt erahh. Emphathemin. Leeeeeaf. Streethembarin. Eeeeepanuamm."

He purposely remembered the exact syllables I'd used. One use was to humiliate me and poke fun at my extreme temporary loss of cognition, and the other reason was because he knew I'd want to document it. I apparently went limp after the fourth inhale.

"You reminded me of a stuttering JFK at one point." Johnny tried to hold in his laughter.

Salvia Divinorum. Diviner's Sage, Seer's Sage or Sally D. One of the most powerful psychedelics known to man and likely the most mysterious. It doesn't work like Psilocybin, Mescaline or DMT. It has no effect on the serotonin receptors but can cause intense, out-of-body introspective hallucinations that can range from approximately two minutes to thirty. Quick, intense and *mindfuckingly transformative*. Due to a prompt legal shutdown in most countries upon discovery, there is a lack of research to know what salvia does to the body, and how it gets you to experience these extremely untameable hallucinations—not only visual but complete physical and audible restructuring of the human brain and vessel. A full-body effect whether you want it or not. It lifts you up, and cuts you down to size. This time, from beginning to end, the *drug* dictates the trip.

I sat up and any after-effects, sensations or anxieties I had were completely stricken from my body. I remembered exactly where I was, who was with me and the seconds leading up to the trip. I turned to Johnny, absolutely mind-blown over the edge of existence.

"I just lived two thousand seven hundred years as a tree," I whispered, trying to hold in the tears and contain my emotion. I wasn't sad, or happy, or had any valid reason to cry, but the overwhelming experience sent my psyche on a rollercoaster that had tipped me over the edge in a matter of a few minutes. I felt broken, torn and reshaped.

Johnny smirked, wondering what the hell I just went through. "What did it feel like? A time lapse? That's a pretty specific number. Why not twenty-five hundred? Why not three thousand?"

"No. No time lapse. I was a legitimate tree, living every second for every one of those years," I tried to explain, knowing he wouldn't fully grasp it unless he experienced it for himself. "My current lifespan is but a single second of what I experienced as this tree. I know it better than I know myself."

Johnny was shocked, rightfully so. This wasn't the usual expectation of a trip. This was far from what either of us had expected, or hoped to experience by any stretch of the imagination.

"How was my breathing in the end?" I asked.

"What?" He was confused.

"You were continuously telling me to breathe." I stared at him, initially thinking he was fucking with me.

"I never told you to breathe." Johnny chuckled. "You were breathing just fine, only a little limp—that's all. I never even spoke until you woke up."

I concluded that it was my conscience telling myself to breathe in a friend's voice. A familiar, trusted presence for me to feel secure and less alone in this uncharted domain. *What else could it have been?*

"Gimme that shit." Johnny snatched the resting joint off the table and gripped his lighter.

I touched his wrist, desperate to make sure he knew what he was getting himself into. "Take it easy. You don't wanna underestimate this, dude. *Not this.*"

I never felt regret over the experience with salvia, but the overwhelming, emotionally confronting effect made me never want to do it again. Johnny took two long inhales, about two less than I did. He smoked a smaller amount because I had the feeling, he wasn't so keen on a three-thousand-year trip. Johnny became stiff, then jerky. His head twitched and I had actually forgotten that he'd just smoked ice about half an hour earlier. I began to panic, wondering how weed, alcohol, ice and fucking salvia was supposed to react inside his feeble body. He twitched again. I expected the worst. I expected foaming from the mouth. I expected a pass-out. I expected a goddamned heart attack.

I began shaking him relentlessly as he seemed to stare vacantly at the ceiling, lifeless with his twitching eyes and massive pupils. His legs jerked back and forth, smacking the underside of the table with force and catching a few eyes around the venue. I continued my attempt to save him by rocking him repeatedly. In retrospect, I may have even worsened the experience for him. I wasn't considering the interpretation of my disturbance on whatever dream state he was in. A single touch of a finger on a heavily tripping person could cause an enormous rupture in their fragile state of mind. Never interfere a tripping friend unless they're in clear physical danger—it could be the difference between a pleasant trip, and a *violently horrific one*.

Suddenly, Johnny's eyes opened. He sat up and took a casual sip of his drink as if nothing had even happened. I hadn't remembered ordering those drinks. Johnny must've ordered them during *my* trip. It was as if he hadn't even inhaled, going from limp to level-headed. He took a deep breath and turned to me with an exhale.

"I am ... *fuckoooked*."

I laughed, but it wasn't amusement. I was relieved that he was alive. "You scared me."

"I went blind, man," he said, staring at the guitarists as they switched with a set of saxophonists. "My body was part of space. A part of the matter surrounding me. It was like another dimension, yet in the same place—but maybe an alternative frequency. The guitars in the background were warped and they vibrated and repeated all around me as if they played the same riff again and again and again. The music was the only thing that followed me through to the other side. I now know what it feels like to be physically stomped into a dot and stretched into eternity."

Johnny had a slamming high and for a second, I thought that maybe it even interacted well in conjunction with all the other shit in his system and music thrown on to garnish. A few seconds later, Johnny's face immediately switched from relief and wisdom to wide-eyed nausea. He turned and vomited his guts out beneath the booth table. I think it was for the best. Any lingering chemicals were just waiting for him to sleep before they were to ambush his body overnight.

We finally left Somersby Lane and headed back to the apartment. I walked in, took a twenty-second shower, brushed my teeth, dropped my clothes and got into bed. Johnny walked in through the door, fell face-first onto the couch and was out for the count.

*

Two weeks passed in Amsterdam, and I'd barely left the apartment. I hadn't touched a substance since that night because I couldn't stop thinking about the tree. *The goddamned tree.* A million thoughts must've gone through my mind, even the same thoughts over and over. It wasn't like mescaline, where I knew I was tripping, where I saw time fly by in flashes and closed-eyed visuals. My current vessel of skin and flesh didn't exist during this trip. I felt that I actually embodied the life of a tree, and felt exactly as *it* felt, and the emotion it endured after watching the world around it grow, live, thrive and then burn to the ground in an abrupt occurrence. It conveyed a story, maybe even a warning. I wondered if I'd just had a major vision and premonition of the world before me and after me. This tree had outlived us all and watched all of humanity begin and go by. Even deeper thoughts triggered, making me wonder if this tree actually exists in the real world, and if I'm living in modern times and it's surpassing the world I'm living in, then that tree could possibly be rooted somewhere on Earth, wherever it may be, and my consciousness inside that trip itself would eternally be living within that tree because I'd already lived another life inside of it. I know, it's confusing. I know, it's absurd. *I can't let it possess my mind like this. It's unfathomable to believe any of it. It just felt so real.*

It's difficult to explain and quite puzzling to comprehend. The thoughts consumed me. A trip that lasted maybe three and a half minutes had me rethinking and questioning a lifetime of living—better yet, two thousand seven hundred years of living. *Had I seen the future through this bout with salvia? Was the modern world the last relic before Earth's imminent destruction and collectively the end of the tree's life?* It could have been simply showing me the whole world through how I generally perceive it, up until the current stage of the world we're living in—and showing the demolition and destruction of everything that surrounds us, the trauma and anguish that Earth had been enduring due to our toxic human existence. Although no words had been spoken by any being during the trip—physical or spiritual—I received messages from something I could only refer to now as Salvia (the aforementioned female presence) that was begging me to understand what we're doing to the Earth and how something needs to change to avoid the imminent collapse of our civilisation. I wasn't only seeing life through this tree. I wasn't only feeling the emotions and pain that this tree felt. I *was* that tree, and it left me in a zone of fear, awakening and absolute exhaustion of my brain post-trip. This was the most powerful experience I'd ever had at this point in my entire life, sober or not. It was a terrifying trip—figuratively and literally out of this world.

All I could do was listen to music and stare in awe at the view we had from our apartment, overlooking a river that ran through the city. After an experience like this, you realise that you must stop sometimes and breathe, take a second to absorb your surroundings, look for the beauty in nothingness, gather and organise your thoughts. I guess it's a form of meditation.

Johnny was in and out, passing by every day, going out and coming back. This part of the stay felt more like a time lapse than the tree trip itself. I wondered where Johnny was going, who he was meeting and how many friends he'd made. A week later, we both decided on Spain, with a few stops along the way. Johnny had a wish to see Italy, and I wanted to stop by Austria and France. On the way to Spain, we agreed: *No hard drugs. Only alcohol and bud.* Sightseeing was the top priority and a chance for a well-deserved break and a period of detoxification. The only problem was, Johnny brought an uninvited guest for the road.

Chapter 10

Only a week into our lofty apartment stay in Ottakring, Austria, I knew something was up with Johnny. At breakfast, he wouldn't speak. At dinner, he'd be easily distracted by the TV's sudden fluctuation in peak volumes. At coffee, his hands would be shaking as if he'd already had three.

September 9th

The apartment was a cosy, yet spacious one with bright red curtains and a real mahogany dining table—not that cheap shit we get back home. It was quite possibly the cosiest stay we had on the trip, but the relationship between Johnny and I was quite the contrary.

"I'm going out." Johnny snatched his coat and headed for the door.

I looked up from washing the dishes, only being a few since Johnny had barely been eating. "Where, now?"

"Do I need to explain myself?" He shrugged.

"Well, yeah." I nodded. "If you're trying shit without me, you gotta tell me. *I'm* writing this story, not you." I turned off the water, drying my hands.

"Are you fucking kidding me?" He gave me a look as if I'd just told him to fuck himself.

I shook my head and moved over to his wallet. "I didn't mean that—you know what I meant, Johnny—" I picked up the wallet because I didn't need him blowing all our cash. Some of mine was in there too, because we'd only bring one when we went out, in case we were to be mugged or something.

"I just need some time alone," Johnny said, staring angrily at the floor and tightening his fist. "Are you gonna stop me from doing *that*, too?"

"What are you talking about?" I yelled. I felt attacked as if he'd just accused me of holding him hostage. "Was it the salvia? Did you experience something you're not telling me about?" It was the only viable reason considering his sudden switch in attitude.

"Get off my back, Clark. Gimme my wallet." He held his hand out, shaking. At this point, I noticed the dark lines beneath his eyes. *I should've paid more attention.* He was acting like a junkie and beginning to look like one. His attitude was almost comparable to that of somebody who was trying to escape some cruel Japanese gangsters.

"You're not getting it back until you tell me where you're going, Johnny." I held the wallet tight.

"You're gonna control me now, too?" He clenched his teeth. "It's *just* like you."

I shrugged, backing away. "The fuck are you talking about?"

He aggressively pointed at me. "You pulled me out of uni." He moved closer. "You made me ditch my family and come out *here*—"

"You're talking shit, man. You need some sleep. That's what you need," I said, on the brink of taking offence. "This is *our* experience—together."

Johnny's eyes started to water, as if his life depended on going out that night. "You're using me. Because you didn't wanna do this yourself!" he yelled, tears quickly streaming. "I had a *life* over there, I had work lined up!" He continued to point at me. "You've pulled me away from everything, and for what? *Drugs?* To get fucked off your brain? I had better things to do!"

I shook my head, raising my palms. "Johnny, it's work, it's journalism—"

"It's bullshit!" He flailed his arms, as if he'd just realised that he'd wasted his whole life. "It's an excuse to go on an adventure and get shit-faced because *you* have nothing better to do with your life."

Appalled at his accusations, I tried to explain. I tried to find reason. "You're not hearing what you're saying, Johnny." I pointed at my folders, books and pens. "I've been writing this shit down for a reason—"

"You're bored, Clark. I know it. Your *family* knows it. You pulled me into this shit because you were selfish and didn't think about me or the consequences this decision had on my future!" He sat down from the stress he'd endured from his rant. His legs couldn't hold him anymore. "You knew I'd be too spontaneously excited to decline. My uncle offered me a job back home, Clark. I turned him down because of this bullshit trip!"

I walked over to him, imploring him to think straight. He wasn't in the right mindset. "Johnny. I'm not bored. This was a legitimate plan—it's all documented. I don't see *you* writing anything down! So, *of course*, it doesn't feel like work to you!" I said, stern.

He stood up. I expected him to come to his senses, maybe even give me a hug and light a smoke to cool off, knowing he wasn't in any state to go out. "You're a shitty friend." He pointed directly in my face. "And you're withholding my wallet. I wouldn't have come with you if I knew you were gonna act like this."

I stared at him for a few seconds. *Where did these feelings come from? We'd been having such a good time up until this point.* It didn't make sense and as much as my decision to drag him along may have been slightly selfish, I thought it was benefitting the both of us.

"Now, give me my fucking wallet, Clark."

I dropped the wallet onto the table and went to bed, unable to sleep. In bed, I listened out for the door and eventually he left into the night.

He yearned to be out of the apartment, as if staying at home and resting meant three hours of searing, blazing incineration in the deepest depths of hell while being whipped with a python by the Devil himself.

I had no experience of tourism during our Austria stay like I'd planned—partly because Johnny hadn't been around to draw me out of the apartment, and I still hadn't quite recovered from the salvia trip. Johnny didn't return for days on end, and even when he came back, it was to get sleep and head out again after a few hours. I had a hunch that it wasn't the sightseeing he'd been so desperately craving.

*

I was able to reclaim a little sanity during this stay, video calling Zoe and discussing my trip with her. We'd only talk around midnight, between Europe falling asleep and Australia waking up. I felt she'd understand better than anyone, whereas Johnny was in no state to confide in. Sure enough, I felt a weight lifted off my shoulders as I unloaded it onto our multiple conversations, analysing it over the phone and dissecting the symbolism and metaphysical messages manifested in my head on this magnificently terrifying substance.

"A tree. It's so stagnant, so mundane, yet such an unbelievably powerful message," Zoe shifted her hair in deep thought. I was never one to video call but if it meant seeing her face, I wouldn't want it any other way. She'd just sit there, biting her nails while I explained the trip. *Nasty habit*, but it was just like her to make it elegantly picturesque. "Promise you'll do it with me one day." She looked up with a piercing stare. "Just once."

"I don't know about that." I sighed, distracted by some cooking show in the background on how to make a soup called *Grah*. "I don't regret doing it, but I just don't think I ever want to do it again. It's entirely another level of psychedelic."

Truthfully, I was grateful to talk to somebody from home, especially because I loved the sound of Zoe's creaky, yet soft voice in the morning—it was soothing and felt partly as if I were lying beside her in bed. Much of the time, when you describe some kind of eye-opening experience to somebody, they either nod and smile, or believe it's simply a chemical reaction and something your brain experienced through another source—as if I'd seen or thought about the tree earlier that same day and the idea had manifested into my trip. Even if that were true, it wouldn't explain the sense of spirituality and unity that came with it. Zoe understood; in fact, she was intrigued and implied that I elaborate. Even other people's trips are sometimes enough to open your own eyes.

When homesick, or on any journey like this, the best way to feel better is to keep in touch with home itself. The worst feeling is the sense that the world's moving on without you. I was even able to treat myself to some bubble baths and avoid smoking, drinking and using altogether. There were two things right about this approach. Firstly, it was a cleanse, some kind of detoxification that allowed me to feel clean, healthy and revitalised. Secondly, when you stay away from that stuff for so long and you relight the fire after a while, each drug, each drink and each smoke tends to hit you just as good, if not *better* than it did the first time.

Meanwhile, Johnny was living the complete opposite life. He'd brought two girls home with him on the penultimate night of the stay. But these weren't Johnny's usual picks. And no, this time, these girls weren't lost, seeking sanctuary, or running away from anybody. They looked a little off. Nervy and skeletal, caked makeup and their eyes (the main tell) were extra baggy with pupils darting in all directions, giving off signs of withdrawal and paranoia. Johnny wasn't having sex with these women—at least, it wasn't his initial intention if he *had* done so—but he was smoking ice with them. Ice has a very distinct scent when smoked. It has a chemical odour, accompanied by sweet undertones. After smelling it once on Somersby Lane, I couldn't mistake that smell for anything else. I decided to leave him to it, hoping it was just a phase—a few weeks of enjoying something all-consuming before moving on to the next thrill and sticking to the agenda. I couldn't tell him how I felt about it—I didn't want to spark up another argument.

*

While giving the apartment a quick once-over before packing our bags and moving on, I noticed Johnny's laptop had been left on the coffee table and wondered if he'd been researching his substances. I was hoping to gain some insight on what he was going through, at least to understand or lend a hand in any way without approaching it directly due to the short length of his current fuse. Instead, I came across an Excel document with lines upon lines of typing. He appeared to have tried another drug in Amsterdam before coming to Austria. Without informing me, he documented it on whatever application he could type it in which happened to be an Excel spreadsheet for some reason. It appeared as follows:

Johnny's Experience: August 24th - 6:22PM

One pill, taken orally. Going to wait a bit. Clark is currently recovering from a trip with what we're referring to now as Sally D, which is why I'm going it alone. Maybe a glass of water will speed up this process. A full glass downed and only a ham and cheese croissant consumed at lunch.

SET: Feeling good. Feeling independent and content with myself. Travelling has been jolly good fun, a little frantic but at least there's time to reflect. I miss home sometimes. But I'm feeling pretty cheerful.

SETTING: Gabriel's apartment. He's out at work and told me to stop over today and try this. I should introduce him to Clark. People are friendlier here. I'm currently alone.

Half an hour has passed. Feeling a bit sluggish and light-headed. Maybe a little nausea from the dose.
One hour: Nausea has completely faded away and I'm feeling quite relaxed. I wanna talk to someone. Feeling lonely. Dry mouth - water is tasting really good right now. I choked a couple times but I feel the water running down my body. It's nice.

maybe two hours? idk. Fingers are numb feeling wavy and airy. I weigh nothing right now. Wait now im sinking. Better close my eyes. My heart rate is much slower. My heads warm

Two and a half? Every time i looke at the clock it's the same time haha is it broken idk i kinda wish clark was here this is feeling real good really really good omg super good kind of anxious
god fuckin knows how much time passed at this point it could be half an hour it could be 33 but jesus crispy my face feels like fucking water. Its littelreal literally water what the actual fuck how do i decribe fthis

=having toruble typin at tshi poin. My finger s arent
hitting the right keys . Wait i think i got it//. I had
tto learn again this feeling is amazing euphoria
I wanna be myself. Im sick fo being evrrythingeverone
and all the world wants me to be. I dont wanna do this
anymore. Im having fun here and people want me back home
working   and   studying   and   working   and   studig
. . . .

feeling kinda horny

it feels really good to type right now i honestly feeling
like i could keep typing keep on typing this is amazing
i wish i could say how i feel in words but words cant
express it panda express it omg i just wanna keep typing
and typing holy mother of god this is honestly a new peak
im rolllllllllllllling right now honestly it feels so
good to type the word honeslty honestly in all honesty

I need to get riff to pay me back for the stuff remnider
to remind me is that his real name? FUCKIGN dweeb

Why cant i feel like this socially why cant i feel happy
all the time why is there a block in the human system
that csuses us to feel like shit msot of the time i just
wanna be happy as happy as i am now why cant i just be
happy. Clark says im the sociable one yeah right if i
was this happy all the time i wouldnt need anrythig or
anyone around me

teeth are gridning and eyes doing werid movments i
honestly honestly thought this would happen sooner
I should call him i dont wanna disturb him i need to talk
need to talk to him i need to speak i cant only type i
need to speak to somebody now i feel cold then i feel
hot i might stop typing soon

So many thoughts flying through my mind now i thought
the last peak was the big one no this is next level shit
im thinking twice about finding someone to talk to becase
i dont wanna lose these rushing thoughtsin my brain

theyre so valuable so so priceless honeslty honestly ;

When your jacket gets caught in something the only way is to pull back and move again or risk ripping the material

begingnign to zone off in space and let my body take flight,/ colours areoun me gettng brightter its gorgeus having trouble spellign but i think its been happenning for a while.

I dont feeel bad anymore i dont need friends why do i need drugs to feel this way why cant we naturally feel this good to be ourselves i fucking love myself but not in a cocky way its self love and value this is what ive been missing.
Italians.
why are they so good why are drugs so good but i dont wanna them to be good i shoulndt need it to feel this way. HA HA HA HAAH HA What the bloody hell is that?

I just got up for a glasss of water and it felt like my body was the water walking through this weird lookig apartment .. why do i need water when i am water? the fuck.
Why why why why why why why why Delilah

horniness returning. i wanna be in love I wish they could love me for who i really am

Vibrations all up and down my body now this is better than sex even the mental part without the physical is still better than sex omg it's like a full body and mental orgasm
I love the feeling of teeth gridning its like ectasy very very similar maybe its the same thing i might jsut sit down for a bit i dont want the effects to escape

Typing is only the surface of what im feeling. I want to feel what im feeling now without a fucnkig drug.

lift off

Johnny experienced a substance that he hadn't stated in the report. I left it unedited to display the words exactly as I had read them. I was quite impressed with his approach as we hadn't yet considered typing the effects and experiencing them in real time. It was a little amusing considering his progressive lack of vocabulary and typing skill while under the influence but in contrast, I was intrigued by the insight into Johnny's psyche and the mental/physical effects he endured. It almost felt like I'd read his diary considering some of the darker places his mind veered to—mostly things I wasn't aware of, and things I hadn't even contemplated. On the surface, Johnny was a highly sociable character, known to build an indestructible concrete wall around his feelings, and most would agree, but this report helped shed light upon some part of his true self, which left me with more respect for him. He wasn't avoiding me in Amsterdam, he just didn't want to bother me after my salvia trip. I had a new sense of appreciation for him.

I later informed Johnny about reading this report and he admitted that he felt a little naked but was more than happy to contribute to the cause. He also mentioned that he wanted to type more but had so many ideas, thoughts and opinions surging through his mind that it was difficult to maintain a constant thought process, especially with his typing capabilities at the time. He wanted to continue and write paragraphs but decided to let himself sink into the trip in free thought. I asked him what substance it was, but he never gave me a straight answer—truthfully, I think he'd forgotten. After some research, the obvious suspects were MDMA, Ethylone or some other variant of empathogen. But he distinctly remembered never having heard of it before, so we assumed it was Ethylone or something we both hadn't yet discovered.

The Excel trip report was typed in Amsterdam, before Johnny's strange dealings and odd behaviour, so we still had a problem on our hands. The debrief in the above paragraph was discussed much later into our journey which was why Johnny was able to divulge his experience. At this point in time, in Vienna, the only two words out of Johnny's mouth seemed only to be: Cash and Quick.

On our last day in Austria, Johnny was driving a hired car and ran over a fire hydrant in the centre of Vienna. He asked me if I could take the fall for it, so that he didn't get drug-tested or lose his licence. This was yet another punishment for being clean and sober. He ran back to the apartment, only a block away, just to get me to come out and claim that I was driving. I guess his plan worked. He paid the bill, which was super expensive for a fire hydrant that must've been preserved from the 1800s or something, but I knew if he'd collided with another driver or a pedestrian, we wouldn't be out of the woods that easy.

October 3rd

Italy came around and we stayed in Milan. An apartment almost the size of a shoebox. I decided to do a little solo touring of the city while Johnny was stuck in his phase. I had a short list of galleries and museums I wanted to visit. This time around, I was ready to let the sun shine upon my skin again, for the first time since Austria, but my companion seemed to want to stay in his cramped bedroom of the apartment for the duration of the stay.

"I can't wait to see you." Zoe was on her break at the shoe store and had another shift at the bowling alley later that evening. She was running two jobs and complained frequently over the lack of time she had, and that our conversations helped to decelerate the clock a little, enough for her to gather a few thoughts.

I ordered a coffee from a small shop outside the apartment. It was a particularly chilly morning, and I was yearning for the hot coffee to increase my body temperature. "I kinda wish I came with you." Zoe sighed. "I know I have shit going on but how often does someone get a chance to travel and do something like this?"

It made me smile, knowing there was time she'd wished we spent together. "You know I'm coming back eventually. I just don't know when." I received my coffee and the heat from the cup itself warmed my frosty hands. "Think about it, we've got the rest of our lives to travel and make memories."

She giggled, knowing exactly what I was implying.

I wanted to plant the seed; I wanted her to understand that I saw more in her than just a one-time experience. She wasn't a summer love. She wasn't some girl I met and expected never to see again. By mentioning the future, I hoped she'd get the hint that I didn't want whatever we had to end. I wanted to be close to her, and I couldn't wait to bring our relationship to fruition upon my eventual return.

During this period of the trip, it felt more like I was travelling with Zoe in place of Johnny; in fact, I even spoke to her more often.

*

I made a real mess of things when I ventured out alone that night. Johnny was nowhere to be seen and I gained traction again with a taste for tunes and sweat. I hit a club in the city centre, and I don't know how or why—*but the Europeans do it better*. While Johnny was hopefully back at the apartment doing some critical thinking, I was hoping to do some critical *drinking*. Those few days spent alone at the apartment in Austria worked up a certain thirst in me—a thirst for exhilaration.

Before I even stepped into the club, we had to wait outside for a little and I met this girl named Erin. About twenty-eight, she was travelling from Berlin and had noticeable dried tears on her cheeks. I had to ask.

"Are you all right? It seems you've had a rough day."

"My husband didn't want me to go out tonight." She lightly patted her face to conceal the streaks. "He wants me to be home all the time. Fuck him."

One of her friends were handing out pills, and because I happened to have been conversing with her, one of those little white buggers made its way to me.

"That's right. Fuck 'em! Freedom to all." I glanced down at the extremely small pill in my palm. "What's in this?" I asked Erin as the music got louder the closer we approached the entrance.

Erin was gorgeous. Her skin had a slight, silky tan and her lips were supple. She was shorter than me, but her confidence heavily outweighed mine. This wasn't an *experience* for her as it had been for me. To her, this was her life, her days, her nights—her highs and her lows. Partying for these people is living, as living for us down under is work.

"It's methocaine." Erin smiled, taking the pill from my palm and holding it above my tongue. "Don't worry. It's not what you think."

As I downed the pill, I thought what *you'd* be thinking. A mix between some kind of crystal meth and cocaine. The cocaine part of it was correct but the meth part derived from methoxetamine (MXE)—similar to ketamine but a slow release, yet more potent and longer lasting. Mixed with cocaine, this night was set to be a hell of a ride. Another thing about these Europeans—they're naturally so much more inclusive, and far more likely to offer you a taste of their drugs.

After stepping into the nightclub and all its bustling music, I think I deserved to have a good experience on a stimulant, seeing as last time the coke was mixed with mescaline, and the dissociative experience was during a heroic case of saving a poor girl from some dropkick in Thailand. I deserved this, and I'd waited long enough. The cocaine kicked in after about twenty minutes as it had been ingested rather than snorted. My body and my mind, conversing in synchronisation. I simply desired to dance, shake my head and shoulders in tandem to the music and the next thing I knew, I was holding hands with Erin. We were feeling the exact same thing, the exact same effects in real time, together. Our bodies felt like one and that may have been an after-effect from my experience with salvia and what it taught me, but it was as if the chemicals were synced in our bodies, rushing through our veins at the same pace, on the same wavelength.

"Feelin' it yet?" Erin smiled. "I know *I* am." She stared into my eyes with an unrivalled seductive expression. I didn't need to break away from her eyes to notice the smile upon her glossed lips.

The music and chemicals ran through my bloodstream quicker than the blood itself. "Oh, *ffffucking* yes, I am." I started laughing at the pure charge of energy this drug had provided me with.

The cocaine seemed to last a lot longer, another effect of it being consumed orally—and that goes with any drug. Finally, after a few drinks, I thought I'd be exhausted after losing myself on the dance floor within the crowd for a half hour straight—then the Mexxy kicked me up to eighth gear. My world spiralled and it felt as though I was viewing my surroundings through a long tunnel. A scope, perhaps. A tingling, quivering sensation ran up and down my legs, up my spine and to the back of my neck. I felt like raw energy, on the same plane as the oxygen that'd been embracing me, in tune with the music, even though I was getting that same feeling I felt on ketamine. It was the atmosphere I needed. It made all the difference this time. Everybody in the club moved in perfect harmony with the music, as if they were a physical representation of the soundwaves. It was a feeling of connection, unsurpassed beauty and telepathic unison, which was likely felt by nobody else aside from the group I'd come in with.

My vision was like watching an old film at a low frame rate. My eyes would slowly follow where my brain had instructed them to look, and everything I saw was in flickers, slowly revealing itself upon my brain requesting the information. It went from chugging a vodka-orange, back to the dance floor with Erin's friend, Adriano, who provided the pills. Back to the bar, ordering a couple drinks for—I don't remember who—then back to the dance floor again. I stood among the crowd with both beverages in hand—double parked—I swiftly downed both drinks and found myself in front of Erin. Then I remember her lips on mine, and I immediately felt filthy, disgusting, plagued with guilt. *I recalled her mentioning a husband.* I didn't stop. Erin held my face, and I couldn't pull away, I didn't want to—especially when I'd melt at the sensation of her long nails caressing the back of my neck to send tingles all the way down to my lower spine. It was as if those chemicals in our veins had forged a magnetised bond between the two of us. It was terribly wrong, but it felt as though we had to do this—we weren't allowed to stop, our bodies wouldn't let us. My brain was screaming at me, urging me to think of Zoe. I shouldn't have been doing this horrible, horrible thing. And blaming anything on a substance is a coward's way out.

I once again split up from her and was beginning to come down from the drugs. The nausea from the alcohol swept in like a sharp breeze, and I decided to sit down. The guilt only swelled as the substances wore off. Adriano approached and slipped me another pill.

"Round two is always *wild*, Amico," he said with his Italian accent and grinned. I downed the pill with ease, hoping to leech onto the fleeting high, possibly to distract my mind from this sudden trench of guilt I'd slipped into. He must've noticed how burnt out I was, and that I needed the pick-me-up. I wondered why I'd already been sobering up after being there for barely three hours. I decided to blame this on the cocaine factor and hoped to reignite the rest of my night.

It took hold almost immediately this time. Some fusion of a placebo effect and a supercharged dose of methocaine, I stood up and searched for Erin. I needed to fix this. I had this sudden idea that if I danced with her without any hint of attraction or making out with her, it should prove to her and prove to myself that it meant nothing and *means* nothing. Before I knew it, I noticed her kissing somebody else and I should've been relieved, but I instead felt betrayed. I can't explain it, I can't understand why these emotions were erupting inside me. By nature, I'm a jealous person and I guess under the influence it's magnified but I shouldn't have been affected this way. I should've left it alone. I shouldn't have taken that second pill. The last thing I remember at the club is dancing with her, while she was dancing with this guy she'd been making out with. It would've made him feel uncomfortable, as if in competition with me, and it would've made Erin feel terribly awkward for these two guys to now be in the same vicinity, virtually competing for her after pashing with her at separate times in the same night. *What the fuck came over me?*

I woke up at 8 a.m. in Erin's bed—nose blocked, and a dry mouth with a wretched taste. I hadn't even remembered having sex with her, but I could tell I'd ejaculated within the past few hours. My body felt spent and beaten. I just wish I remembered how we got to that point and what happened to that other guy. My knuckles pained for some reason but I don't remember getting into any fight. My hands were more so scraped, as if they'd been dragged on concrete. The morning headache was the worst I'd ever had.

"I need to call my husband." Erin groaned, sliding out of bed and snatching her bra. She couldn't even look at me.

Before I could sit up and rethink the decisions from the night before, there were two loud thumps at the door. Erin turned to me, wide-eyed. The knock was heard again, and a man spoke. I couldn't understand him. He was speaking Italian, but he was calm and seemed to be apologising.

She desperately whimpered, "There's a back door. Please?"

I was the antagonist. She'd never done this before. I could see the fear, the shame and the guilt in her eyes. Her life, and the life of the man waiting outside—was about to capsize. I headed quickly over to the back, catching a glimpse of the man waiting at the door with a worrisome expression. He loved her, and obviously wanted to make it work. It couldn't get any worse than this ... then it did.

He had a fucking child. He had a little girl with him. She was about four or five with a pink Cinderella backpack, excited to see her mother for the first time in likely a week. *What did I just do to this family?*

I didn't know. I promise, I didn't fucking know.

*

I decided to head back to the apartment and set our destination to France. From what I remember, this was the first time I lacked memory from a night out. I later read that memory loss was a potential side effect with ketamine—I figured it must've been the same with MXE.

I reached the apartment and noticed Johnny smoking a glass pipe in the lounge but he had a new friend with him. The dude was hunched, super skinny with long hair, yet not much of it. His teeth were notably orange-yellow. Easily thirty-five years old.

"Who the fuck is this?" I stared at Johnny and gestured to the stranger in our apartment. My brain required rest and recalibration after the night I'd had—not a surprise like this.

"This is the *guyyyy!*" Johnny pointed to me with squinted eyes. *Shit*, I thought. *What information has he told this stranger about me, and about us?*

The man threw his chin up at me, attempting a friendly welcome. "Ciao, I'm—"

"I wasn't asking you," I continued, staring at Johnny, ignoring this junkie in my apartment.

Johnny shrugged, "Clark, meet Lagos. Been meaning to introduce you guys."

Lagos smiled, thinking I'd be gracious with this warm welcome, smoking ice in my temporary residence. "A pleasure to greet you, Clark," he said in his broken Italian accent.

They both started giggling, as if they'd expected this reaction from me, as if they'd shared prior conversations about it. "Get up, we're packing our things," I said sternly.

Johnny looked puzzled. "Where're we going? What's the next destination, *Captain?*" he comically puffed his chest like a sailor.

I looked over at Lagos, knowing he'd follow us. "Just pack your shit, Johnny. This has gone too far."

I didn't have to guess twice to understand that Johnny had made friends with a meth-head. He seemed his normal, conversative self again, which for me was worrying, considering this new dingbat was now part of the equation, squatting in our apartment. Maybe he gave Johnny what he wanted: *a fix*.

Johnny had found himself in the treacherous depths of an addiction. If this was the case, I'd be blaming myself for dragging him onto this trip with me. Immediate action needed to be taken. The next morning, I decided we were moving on to Spain—thus skipping France. The reason was to get Johnny as far from Lagos as possible. When you've got an addiction to a drug, you tend to mistake the people who provide them to you as dear friends. Lagos wasn't Johnny's friend. He had no money and no place to stay, so when Johnny came around with a pocket full of cash and a yearning for something sweet—enter Lagos, carrying nothing but connections.

We needed to continue our quest for substances, which, I thought, might just help break any underlining addiction that Johnny may have found himself in. One hundred times I must've asked myself if this was only an excuse to fuel the resumption of our journey. Maybe it was a way for me to silence those lingering thoughts about that family in Milan, and the damage I'd left in my wake.

As for Johnny, I hoped that if I'd introduced something new to his system, then he may not feel the itch for what I'd confirmed was a rapidly developing ice addiction. But in the back of my mind, I was left to contemplate, was it the right approach to send a python out to kill a cobra? This was getting ugly, quick, and I needed a solution, fast.

It's easy to outrun fear, but how far can you really get when you're running from yourself?

Chapter 11

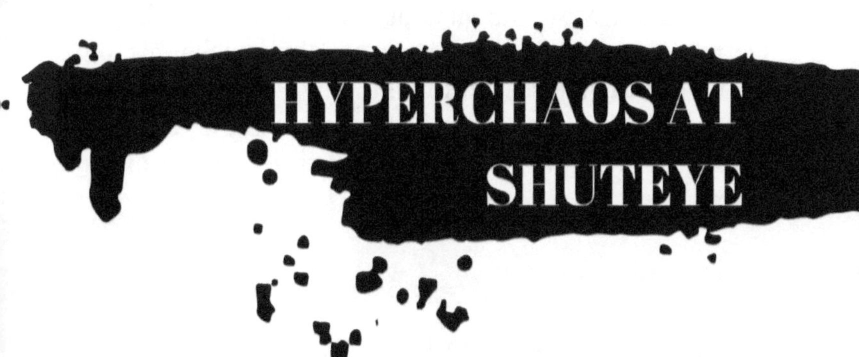

"Why'd we skip France?" Johnny lifted his head from the train window. "Where the hell are we?" Lazy-eyed, he'd been out cold the entire trip, covering his eyes from the harsh rays of the Andalusian sun. Luckily, during slumber, he was able to block out the incessant wailing of a toddler occupying one of the seats ahead with an inconsiderate mother that couldn't care less.

"Spain," I said, collecting our things. "We're in Granada." I was surprised he was even physically able to make the trip.

"I wanted to see Paris," Johnny said under his breath. On account of my distrust, I assumed he informed Lagos about France and expected to rendezvous there. A good call on my end. *Sometimes, the gut is to be trusted.*

I placed my hand on his shoulder with a reassuring smile. "This place is like the old Middle East, but cooler—you should feel right at home."

I was reluctant to give him a straight answer. I was afraid he'd think I just banned his newfound 'friend'. We'd already had a previous spat about my control over this trip and I wasn't about to pry open that can of slippery worms. I also didn't want to make it obvious that his junk addiction was the reason for skipping France, especially when he hadn't the courage to voice it to me himself. I needed to straighten it out rather than let this thing run rampant.

*

We stayed down south in Granada, out of the city in a small town, in a three-bedroom house. I deliberately chose a place ten minutes from the city to get Johnny away from the street dealers. This time, I oversaw where we went, and he couldn't get far without alerting me. I wondered if my desperate measures were overstepping the bounds of our friendship as Johnny had previously accused—but whatever it took, I wasn't letting him be consumed by a substance, especially if my journalism was the reason for it.

Before I knew it, he was getting scratchy again. Johnny's eyes had become sunken and dark, and you could tell his head wasn't in the right place. Within three days, he copped two blood noses—one of which he attempted to hide from me.

"What's that noise?" He looked around, grinding his teeth, irritable. "Is someone out there?"

Cold turkey was the difficult way to deal with this, for him and for me, and most likely wouldn't work. He'd sooner go mad.

"There's nobody there, Johnny. It's a quiet place." I nodded while pouring him some tequila—the last 150 ml of our stock. "Go back to sleep."

His restless mind wouldn't doze off, and his dinners were left uneaten. If he wasn't smoking a pipe or on the hard booze, he'd just sit there all day, his brain waiting for the next ounce of mind-altering particles to enter its system. Alcohol wasn't fulfilling its duty as a distraction as we had initially intended; instead, it seemed to contribute to the process, likely increasing the damage on my dear friend. I needed to get my hands on something quick, anything accessible that might steer him from this horrible path he'd found himself on. We needed a diversion, something that induces a different state of mind. Zoe advised that this strategy helps with killing addiction.

October 21st

I trekked into town in search of magic mushrooms, finding myself in the nearby forest and wetlands to claim them fresh, but had no such luck. I then ventured into Granada to see if anybody could at least direct me to find them. Laws on these things are much looser around these parts—not legal per se, *but less controlled.* I wasn't successful in my search, but I did come across a man, Juan, who claimed to be a Psychonaut (a person who dabbles regularly in psychedelics) and he mentioned a plant nearby that gave off a pretty *great* high, and all I had to do was harvest its sharp and spiky pods by snipping them, prying them open and consuming the seeds inside. He called it 'datura'. He mentioned that it'd work wonders for my friend and that I've never tried anything quite like it. The upside was that it was free. For me, this solution sounded perfect and affordable. *I wish I'd done my homework first.*

On the way back to the house in Granada, I was excited to try these potent seeds after hearing all the rage about them from a local. I needed to somehow distract my friend in need with something powerful—powerful enough to cut a sweeping addiction. It seems all that time I spent in the apartment in Amsterdam, he was out there consuming the same shit every night. I made an executive decision to ingest the seeds in the safety of the house we rented and given Johnny's physical condition, it seemed like a safe bet.

When I returned to the house and hung my coat on the rack, I noticed a traveller's backpack in the hallway—it wasn't Johnny's, and it sure as hell wasn't mine. After hearing a faint Italian accent echo through the hallway, I knew exactly who'd come to visit. I stomped into the lounge room where Lagos had been sipping coffee with a smoke. Johnny seemed himself again—at least, close to what I remembered him to be a few weeks earlier. Obviously, he'd given Lagos the address for a place to stay, in exchange for sharing his ice. This was getting way out of hand.

"What the fuck is going on, Johnny?" I yelled, chucking the unopened pods on the bench.

"Don't be a buzzkill, man," muttered Lagos. "We're almost peaking—"

I snatched the glass pipe from Johnny's hand and passed it to Lagos. He could be as fried as he wanted for all I cared.

"What happened to trying everything once?" I yelled at Johnny. "Ice wasn't even on our fucking list!"

"Dude, it's something I enjoy. I can be done with it whenever I want. Plus, we've tried heaps of shit that wasn't listed." Johnny was about to continue speaking when a wide-eyed Lagos identified the bag of pods.

"Is that what I think it is? You guys are crazier than I thought." He nodded, impressed that we had the balls to try this shit. Somehow, he knew what they were.

"I'm gonna need you to leave." I pointed Lagos to the door.

He stared at me, confused, with a smoke in one hand and a pipe in the other. "You're not going to try that by yourselves, are you?"

"You gotta understand that we're not just junkies travelling the world. We have an agenda and you're fucking it up," I said, stern.

"I can understand that." Lagos shrugged. "But you're gonna need a trip sitter."

"And *you're* gonna be that person?" I raised an eyebrow, staring at something of a slack jaw.

"I've had my fix for today. And not in a million years am I trying *that* shit." He sat back, seemingly calm.

I should've known better to trust somebody I didn't know. I should've kept an eye on him. I ripped four pods off the plant which contained about a hundred and fifty seeds each. Again, none of us were experienced with datura, not even Lagos. And for good reason. Johnny was prepared. Any distraction from sobriety seemed like a good one.

"I say we take about one fifty seeds and see how it pans out," I suggested to Johnny.

Johnny nodded and Lagos chimed in, "Crack them open and I can brew the shells into tea. If the effects don't come on, you can drink it." he said with a convincing smile. An apparent expert botanist.

To me, that sounded like a sure trip, so Johnny and I chewed down fifty bitter-tasting pods. We then decided to swallow the remaining hundred whole to avoid the awful texture. Lagos had already begun boiling the pod shells on the stove with a few of the datura leaves that I'd additionally harvested. A mysterious psychoactive drug in the vicinity of a meth-head boiling a pot on the stove.

What could possibly go wrong?

*

T+2 HOURS:

Not a single change or sensation had been experienced aside from a little sweat and exhaustion. I looked over at Johnny on a recliner chair in the corner of the room and he shrugged. Lagos decided to take some for himself, considering it had little to no effect on us in the first couple of hours. We sipped the tea, consuming about half a cup each. My perception of time may be scattered or inaccurate, but I tried my best to place these memories in the order of what I could recall.

T+4 HOURS:

As I sat in the lounge room, I felt my mouth become unbearably dry as if I hadn't even had the saliva to soak it with. I hurried over to the sink and washed my mouth, drinking water to quench my thirst but it was impossible to eradicate the feeling. I even tried to eat a muffin from a packet we'd bought earlier but my mouth was so dry that I couldn't even swallow it. It felt as if my oesophagus were that of a withering corpse.

T+5 HOURS:

Sitting on the couch, I soon forgot about my thirst because I noticed a stain on the ceiling move slightly. Small legs appeared and it crawled across the plaster above. Then came another one, and another, swarming the ceiling until the white paint was covered by all these black bugs. I lit a cigarette. I don't know whose it was, but it was *just* what I needed. As I smoked it, it soon disappeared into thin air, and I realised I was never actually holding a smoke at all. I felt stupid and shook my head, looking around for a real cigarette.

"Do you know where the cigarettes are?" Johnny asked the exact question I was about to ask him. For a second, I believed he spoke telepathically.

I replied, "I was just about to ask you the same question."

Johnny didn't respond at all. I even waved in his face, and he stood completely still, as if a cardboard cut-out. "Dude, are you fried?" I asked with a nervous giggle, wondering how somebody could sit so still for so long. I thought he was playing some kind of trick on me.

Johnny disappeared. I wondered if he'd run away, possibly tripping so hard that he needed to vomit. *Maybe I offended him somehow?* I got up to find him, feeling incredibly drunk and disorientated before noticing Johnny sitting on the couch in the exact same position he was in before. *Did I imagine that conversation with him?* I took a drag of my cigarette. Then, I realised I had the cigarette and dropped it, wondering where the hell it came from, and where the hell it went. I kneeled to the ground to pick it up, but it was gone. It had fallen into some kind of void, impossible to trace among the travelling lines and stains on the patterned carpet. My now hypersensitive fingers were running along the material, feeling for this cigarette as if I were blind. Then, I realised again, I had no cigarettes and wondered how foolish I looked searching the floor for about a half hour—possibly hours—for something that didn't exist.

T+8 HOURS:

I thought this would be the peak of the high; in fact, I'd forgotten I'd taken datura at all at this stage. A party of people showed up at the house. I assumed they were all Lagos' friends and he invited them to keep him company. I felt some form of comfort from these guests and engaged in conversation with most of them, but they all seemed to resemble some version of Sloth from *The Goonies*, not in a comedic sense but more fucked-up, grotesque, mutated and disfigured kinds of faces. Even though these entities were nightmarish, it all felt normal to me as if I knew these people all my life and were one of them. Each person would talk to me, then disappear, then reappear in different places of the kitchen in different clothing or as completely new people. Every time someone disappeared, I felt a great sense of loneliness until the next conversation gained traction.

I eventually found myself talking to Trey, an old buddy of mine from high school. He was always in a green hoodie and had this unmistakeable mischievous smile on his face. I hadn't seen him in years and didn't question the fact that he was, by chance, in Granada.

"The rats are gonna die. The rats. They're going to die." Trey was concerned about these apparent rats that'd been roaming the house. "Sink water, *fast.*"

My new quest was to place the rats in the sink to keep them wet, so they could stay alive. I listened to him, snatching these large, infected and rabies-riddled rats off the ground and piling them into the massive industrial sink of the home, watching a dozen of them squirm and struggle amongst each other until they changed form and flew out of the sink as a swarm of giant moths.

I glanced over at Trey, but he still wasn't satisfied. "They're outside. The rest of them are outside."

Trey disappeared from my sight. I assumed I'd just lost focus and hadn't noticed him walk outside. I hurried through the hallway, desperate to locate him and save these Spanish rats.

"Trey! Don't let them bite you," I yelled. "They've got rabies." I began to worry that he was in some kind of trouble.

I darted straight for the front door and tugged at the handle but it was locked. Upon snatching a conveniently placed key nearby, I jammed it into the doorhandle—but it snapped. Both pieces of the key fell to the floor and as I kneeled down to retrieve them, both ends were wriggling around, pink—it'd become a severed worm. I tried the door handle again, without the key, and this time it turned with ease.

I opened the front door of the house and noticed Trey balancing on the roof outside. "Trey! Get down from there! What the fuck are you doing?" I didn't question anything, and I felt sober, perfectly unaffected by substance. This all seemed entirely casual as if Trey were being his usual idiotic self.

He began tying a noose around his neck. I panicked but was unable to move my feet. They were trapped in some kind of muck-like quicksand. I reached out to Trey and yelled but he jumped off the roof and hung himself from the chimney. I cried for him, helpless to save him but somehow, every time I looked back at him, he jumped again, as if a video of him committing suicide was playing on some kind of endless loop—some kind of gif. It was replaying over and over until I rushed back inside the house to gather my thoughts.

As I sat down on the couch, all those disfigured entities suddenly had no faces. Instead of conversing, they were all having wild, violent, insatiable sex with blood and organs merging and morphing. It wasn't for enjoyment or pleasure, it was like they'd all helplessly become creatures, simply behaving in this manner for the basic natural requirement of population or primal animalistic urges. I tried to ignore them. I even begged for them to keep it down to respect the tragic loss of Trey, but it seemed they just groaned and moaned louder, wilfully ignoring me. I thought about Trey and the fact that he just died, but I then realised that the real Trey died three years ago, eventually leading me back to the reality that I had ingested datura. He didn't commit suicide either—he battled cancer. And come to think of it—this house had no chimney to jump from. I was confused again. *Why is my brain doing this to me?* Everything felt real, and I was believing everything I was seeing. I was in a dream state, dipping in and out of consciousness, as if I were awake, but sleepwalking and my dreams were manifesting into reality. The more stress my brain was under, the more intense these hallucinations were.

The only thing I can compare this feeling to is dreams, and theoretically being able to fly or experience something physically impossible within them—yet not questioning or wondering how or why it's happening. In your dreams, these aspects seem perfectly feasible.

T+11 HOURS:

I awoke in bed, tucked in tight. *Did I do this to myself?* My heart was beating frantically as if it were about to burst.

I heard voices, many of them, thousands of them. "Die", "Overdose", "Heart failure", "He's going to die-die-die". "Shit, shit!"

This drug is going to kill me.

T+14 HOURS:

I came to, in a mahogany bar, mid-conversation with Johnny on the barstools, sitting beside me. He seemed completely normal—the Johnny I remembered from back home. The bartender looked at me, confused. I couldn't speak Spanish but even if I did, I don't think my brain was functioning enough to understand *anyone* that spoke to me. He was gesturing to the chair beside me, yelling something strange. I wanted to smoke another cigarette, but I knew they wouldn't take too kindly to me lighting up indoors. I picked up a shot of Scotch that had been previously placed in front of me and downed it. After swallowing, I wasn't holding any glass. I wondered if I'd even tasted the alcohol or if I'd imagined it.

I looked over to Johnny. He spoke before me. "There's no drink in this drink. What drink? What glass?" he murmured. He then looked over to me, deadpan. What he said next was the only sentence in this segment that was clear as day. "You're fucked, and your friend is dead." It scared the fuck out of me.

I looked at him in horror, confused over why he was saying these terrible things. I glanced in the mirror behind the bartender to see Johnny's reflection and it was me. I was sitting beside myself but the alternate version of me held this indescribable demonic presence. As if the other version of me were about to do something horrifically barbaric and was just waiting for the second I let my guard down. The paranoia was setting in and I was surely on the brink of psychosis, if not already in the clutches of it.

I had to get out of there, but I couldn't find the door. A Spanish comment was heard every now and then, directed at me. Perhaps they were asking if I was okay. Perhaps, they were telling me to get the fuck out. This bar had no doors. *They're trying to trap us here!* After what felt like twenty minutes, I reached the conclusion that the only way in and out were the bathrooms. I tried to read the signs for male or female, but the letters were all jumbled up. It was alien language; I couldn't make out any words and even the pictures were dancing so much that I couldn't decipher which was male or female. The figures on the doors were diving like dolphins on a loop. I looked at the bar menu to confirm my illiteracy and it was true— the entire menu was incomprehensible. Letters didn't look like letters anymore; it was all squiggles and odd shapes and lines merging together in frustrating fashion. Suddenly I remembered where the door was and quickly headed for it so it wouldn't vanish for a second time. I tried to open it, but it was locked. The door wouldn't budge. I couldn't escape this damn bar and I began banging on the door, trying every which way to get through it. Then I concluded that I was hallucinating. The door wasn't real. It was either already opened or non-existent. I jumped through it—I was right. *Maybe I'm getting the hang of this.*

I found myself walking the streets outside. People I knew from my school life were skipping on the roads and sidewalks, in school uniform, disappearing and reappearing. Obviously, this wasn't possible but at the time, it felt perfectly sound, as if I expected them there. I noticed a tall man wearing a fedora across the street, watching me. He looked suspiciously ominous and I wondered if he was after me. I suddenly believed I was being tested by this man in some way, like he was writing notes about me, and that every move I made was being recorded by him. *He must be here for me! He must be studying me closely to claim my experiences and publish them as his own! He's been stalking me this whole time, this entire trip. He's finally been caught out!*

I called to him, "Hey! What are you looking at? Mind your own business and get a life!"

I walked across the street. There were cars passing me, beeping their horns but going right through me like ghosts. I was invincible, slowly walking across this peak-hour busy road at 4 a.m. in this secluded part of town. I continued calling to him as the man in the fedora and trench coat just stood there, writing his notes, looking up at me, then writing some more.

"Do you hear me? Who are you? I wanna know what you're writing about me!"

By the time I crossed the never-ending road and placed my hand on the man's shoulder, I realised it was just a tall, black streetlight with a loose flamenco flyer attached. I shook my head in confusion. *An utter mindfuck.* I wondered what I looked like to a sober person as I finally remembered yet again that I took datura and tried to ground myself by heading back home, wherever that was.

T+17 HOURS:

I opened my eyes again and I had somehow appeared in the bathroom of the house. I was mid-conversation with a green and gold mantis, about a metre tall, while urinating on the bathroom floor, attempting to put out an invisible flame, although I could barely expel urine.

Johnny was behind me. "Ebleee pissing on tiles—eeeuu fucken drunk bastard—I ate your muffin—was rocks. Vegetable heaven." Johnny didn't make the slightest ounce of sense, but I couldn't tell if he *was* making sense, and I was too fucked to understand it—or if he was simply speaking out of his mind. I decided it was probably a combination of both.

I turned back to continue my conversation with the mantis. I wanted to ask him if my urine was enough to extinguish the flames. I then realised I'd been talking to a fashionable lamp the whole time. *Better piss on it to be sure.*

I turned back to Johnny and gripped him by both shoulders. "Dude, don't ever try this drug. No matter what you do," I implored him. "It's dangerous, horrifically dangerous, mannn!"

I don't know why I was begging him. I already knew he consumed just as much as I did. Johnny then turned, pulled out a joint from his pocket and walked away without saying a single word. This aggravated me for some reason, as if he'd ignored me. I tried to pull up my pants but noticed I wasn't wearing any after the third time of grabbing the invisible trousers from around my feet. I walked out of the bathroom and Johnny wasn't there, but someone else was.

I can barely explain it, but I can attempt to. I saw her, I saw the most breathtakingly gorgeous woman I'd ever seen in my life, smiling at me with a sweet expression and some kind of white glow surrounding her. Her hair was platinum white for some reason, and her face was perfect—indescribably perfect, every feature, jaw-droppingly symmetrical. *God's ideal masterpiece.* She gestured for me to follow her and of course, I did. I didn't want this part of the trip to end. It was as if my consciousness had crafted the definition of perfection and manifested it into a physical being created just for me. I can't recall her precise features, but her presence and aura were the source of her attraction. She politely smiled with a massive sense of love and kindness as I approached her. But before I could touch her, a fat cockroach exited her mouth. *Ew fuck!* I stepped back in fright and noticed another one escape the void between her lips.

"You've got roaches in your mouth!" I yelled, in case she hadn't already noticed.

Suddenly, it wasn't the datura goddess anymore, it was *Zoe*, and she began panicking from the now unbearable number of cockroaches crawling out of her mouth and climbing amongst her teeth.

"Clark, what's happening? What happened to your arm?" she asked while crying. I ignored her words as she fell to the ground in sheer horror.

I watched her scream and struggle as these foul creatures ate her alive from the inside, crawling in and out of her eyes and ears until her hair began morphing into these vicious bugs that could no longer be contained. Her shrieks were deafening me until she couldn't scream anymore because these bugs took over her body like a decaying corpse. Zoe wasted away to nothing, and these cockroaches disappeared, possibly looking for their next victim.

T+21 HOURS:

I woke up and looked at a wall in front of me with scribbles and writing in crayon. I tried to make it out and I was only able to read it because the letters were so big. *'Clark. 22th of October. Datura.'* I caught a glimpse of a memory of Johnny writing it for me because I'd forgotten who I was, what month it was and why I was so fucked up. Johnny wrote those words to remind me of the hallucinations for when I woke up. It helped. I tried to move but I was tied down. My wrist was in tremendous pain, and I looked over at it, drenched in blood, twisted the wrong way. It was broken and needed immediate attention.

I coughed and looked up at Johnny beside me, back in Somersby Lane, Austria. I'd just smoked salvia and placed it between Johnny's fingers. He was smiling uncontrollably for some reason.

"What are you doing to me, Clark?" Johnny's voice sounded distressed, but giggly. "What are you doin'?" He was still smiling like a party clown. *What the fuck is going on?*

Johnny sucked the salvia in and exhaled, placing what now was a purple lollipop onto the table. The jazz music continued, and Johnny's smile disappeared. He was upset and his face grew red, redder than a lobster, redder than a tomato, redder than Betelgeuse. Johnny's head woodified and became something of a tree, growing at a rapid rate.

"I'm sorry, I'm sorry!" I screamed over and over as his head split apart into pieces of wood and grew destructively through the ceiling. "I'm sorry, Johnny! I'm sorry!" *It was all my fault.*

I woke up in the bedroom again. Only ten minutes must have passed, and I read the writing on the wall again. *'Clark. 22ᵗʰ of October. Datura.'*

*

Datura Stramonium. Other names include Thornapple, Jimsonweed, Nightshade, Devil's Snare, Devil's

Trumpets—names intended on reflecting the deadliness behind such a toxic substance and repelling those who seek it. They're usually white, decorative flowering weeds that inflict violently intense hallucinations on the brain. Every aspect of the datura plant is highly toxic and can kill you with ease, sending you on an insanely dangerous trip that can turn a college professor into a fried vegetable in the matter of an hour. It's also massively unpredictable with no benefits whatsoever aside from its use in ancient rituals and ceremonies. Dying it, boiling it, drying it or altering it in any way will never destroy the atropine, scopolamine or hyoscyamine: the tropane alkaloids—its poisonous, hallucinogenic properties. This is *no* psychedelic, and I wish I knew it earlier. This is a deliriant of tremendous power, a subcategory that should never be fucked with, and could turn you into a hostile schizophrenic for three days or forever. An ideal death trap for all those ignorant risk takers and rule breakers. To lose control on a drug is one thing, but to lose yourself is another. The only other deliriants worth noting are chemicals manufactured for human experiments in warfare at Edgewood Arsenal in the US—so, the risk is self-explanatory. This is probably the only real hallucinogen that gives psychedelics a bad name, even though it's not directly classified as one. Psychedelics, if respected, usually have a positive effect on the mind— even after what you may refer to as a 'bad trip'. A deliriant is another animal—it sends you into a total nightmare and even the most seasoned, experienced psychonauts are never mentally prepared for the hellish visions and traumatising encounters that are associated with datura. It's not a mere natural psychedelic—*it's poison.* It's the plant's way to defend itself. It's the plant's way to kill those who killed *it*.

My wrist was fractured and after leaving the hospital in Granada, I went back to the house. A *pigsty* is an understatement. Nearly all the windows were shattered. The sinks were all full of soil and clothes. Broken glass, urine and blood on the floor, objects and ornaments either smashed or placed in unusual locations. Lamps in the freezer, and framed paintings in the bathtub. One of the bedrooms were boarded up like a horde of zombies had attacked the house. Seeing these things induced recollections of the events from the days prior. I remember Lagos trying to attack Johnny as if he'd gone insane and thought Johnny was out to murder him. I figured that Johnny boarded up that room to get away from him. Lagos was naked most of the time, hurling his skeletal body at the boarded bedroom door and slamming his head against the walls, breaking glass and screaming psychotically. Johnny claimed that Lagos was frightened, thinking terrorists were invading the property to slaughter him. Johnny labelled the occurrence as the most mental, clinical and schizophrenic insanity that he'd ever witnessed in any human being. Lagos was possessed by sheer psychosis. I could easily think of at least four reasons why his experience was worse than ours. He's a junkie, so any drug or health problems in his system would have surely interacted negatively with the deliriant. He also has a chequered past—needless to say—which wouldn't have made the hallucinatory imagery anything more desirable or euphoric than ours. His method of administration differed by him brewing a tea, and likely consuming far more than Johnny and I. And finally, it's fucking datura, so anything goes.

I began cleaning, even with sharp headaches, lingering hallucinations and odd sensations that kept fading in and out like invisible stains on the walls and the feeling of ants crawling up my neck. But at this point, I was sober enough to know these sensations weren't real.

For the next few days, I couldn't focus on close objects, my pupils were still dilated, and I couldn't read small print for at least twenty-four hours post-trip, probably longer. Johnny exited that boarded room with scratches all over his face and faeces on the interior walls. He didn't want to talk about his trip, and I think he was genuinely disturbed and horrified over what he saw. I gave him time, hoping he'd talk about it sooner or later, but he didn't. He just shook his head every time I asked. One of the only things he noted about the experience was that his eyesight is permanently damaged. He could no longer read fine print up close. I brushed it off, thinking it would fade away as mine did over a couple days, but his eyesight never recovered. Johnny would need to acquire a prescription for glasses upon our eventual return home.

*

In case anybody thinks datura is going to be anything like salvia, ayahuasca, shrooms, mescaline or acid, they'd be dead wrong—maybe even *dead*. I read up on it during the days of recovery and a lot of what we experienced, interestingly enough, others had, too. The invisible cigarette is a common phenomenon with datura, when you think you're smoking but you're not. The flash forwards to different locations. The grotesque creatures and mindless intercourse. The bugs are also apparently frequently seen throughout these trips, but what hit me the hardest was the most interesting part of it—the gorgeous woman. Many reports of datura had included this perfect, angelic woman and many refer to her as the Greek goddess: Atropos, The Inevitable—the eldest of the three sisters of fate, and known to be the figure of finality, the goddess that severs the life thread to conclude your destiny, the one that sends you into death. The tropane alkaloid in datura: *atropine* was named after this goddess—and for good reason. The female figure that often appears in these hallucinations is well known to be quite comforting, communicating with you in the most attractive way, as the Devil is known to, and sometimes being upset at you for harvesting her precious flowers and abusing its seeds. This was the only spiritual takeaway from the experience.

Datura is poison and I'll forever be affected, frightened and traumatised by it. None of the feelings, emotions or sensations were desirable—I just became a temporarily insane person dreaming in an inescapable double dimension, caught between reality and a nightmare. I wondered what I looked like from an outer perspective. I felt lucky, considering many of the others stories I read post-trip, resulting in users breaking limbs, eating their own hands, dismembering themselves and their genitalia, having heart attacks, drowning, stabbing others, committing suicide and remaining in a state of insanity forever—a complete end to one's life over the simple action of consuming any part of this brutal plant, many of them not even aware of the consequences or the origin of the substance they're even ingesting. Some of them even being persuaded by a friend that it's a form of mescaline, taking it with confidence because some dealer wanted a dollar.

I went for a walk a couple of days later and noticed the damaged door of the bar I found myself in that night, awaiting repair. The door *was* indeed closed during the trip, and I tried to hide my face in case they remembered me. I concluded that barging through that door was how I fractured my wrist, thinking there was no door at all. I realised in retrospect that I was that person who talks to themselves on the street, the person who people point to and say, "That guy's on drugs." A fucking embarrassment. Like I said, datura isn't a psychedelic. I wouldn't even refer to it as a drug, even if it causes hallucinations—it's a poison, a heavily toxic and relentless deliriant, and something that should be avoided at all costs.

*

After a few days, I felt like myself again. Although, a sense of disconnection from the world followed for a few weeks after, eventually evaporating while my physical wrist pain remained.

One other thing Johnny had mentioned from his experience was a number. *2711*. It had no significance, no direction and no meaning but this number was imprinted in his head, and he didn't know why. The number seemed to speak to him during and after his time on datura. It hadn't meant squat to either of us, but to him it was important and something he wouldn't forget—even if he wanted to. I couldn't make sense of it, although I did understand the sudden feeling of importance in something that wouldn't ordinarily be so. Places, visions, words, numbers and experiences can stay with you forever after any trip, especially things that seemingly mean nothing.

I decided to video call Zoe for a debrief. The comedown took a while but I was ready to offload it. Our conversation was quite cheerful at first. We were playfully planning our future.

She thought hard, lying on her bed and twirling her hair, "I can picture you in grandpa slippers, on a recliner, yelling at the TV with a newspaper in hand—and calling teenagers *Whippersnappers*."

Of course, in her portrayal of me, I'd be complaining about something. *I always am.* "Well, I can picture *you* sitting beside me on our big, open porch, reminiscing in a rocking chair over how we met."

"Truly an enchanting tale to tell our grandchildren," She couldn't help but smirk. "Drugs. Real hard drugs brought us together."

I don't know why I thought of that place. The porch and the rocking chair. It was the closing frame of my mescaline experience—except this time, Zoe was a part of it. My mind had somehow defaulted that place to be something I wanted, as if that was where I'd pictured the end of my life to be. Before I could carry on, the conversation took a turn for the worse.

"You hang out with any girls over there?" Zoe asked. I could tell this'd been a question she'd been itching to ask for a while. "I heard the people are more laid-back."

I'm no liar. "Zoe," I sighed. "I have to tell you something and you're not gonna like it."

The eerie silence sent a hundred and forty butterflies into my stomach at once. I even tried my best to dampen the blow by mentioning Johnny's bedscapades, hoping that my night with Erin from Milan would seem minuscule and insignificant. The only problem was, the night was such a blur that I wasn't sure if we'd even *had* sex, other than simply sleeping in the same bed. I wanted to believe we didn't, seeing as it would've been difficult because when you're on most stimulants or empathogens, a man's genitals typically shrink up and render themselves useless—unless it somehow worked its way out of my system before sleeping with her. I seemed to figure this out by explaining it to Zoe while trying to uncover the mystery for myself which wasn't the best approach. Zoe took the stand shortly after.

"You're a fucking swine!" Zoe cried over the phone. By this time, she'd switched the camera off. "I've turned people down for you! I've controlled my urges, Clark! What the fuck?"

"I don't even talk to her," I frantically tried to explain. "It can't possibly mean anything—she has a husband and a kid, Zoe—I don't even know if we *did* anything—"

"A husband, and a child? Are you *sick?*"

I was set to continue, but considering the words exiting my mouth and the monstrous picture I'd been painting of myself ... I decided that speaking would only worsen the matter.

"You're not who I thought you were. I really thought we had something real. What the fuck am I waiting around for?" There was only silence over the phone for a few seconds. Her voice calmed, almost to a whisper. "I don't know how I could ever forgive you." I could hear her muffled sniffles in the background over the black screen. I could only imagine how much I'd hurt her.

How could I do this to such a fragile being?

How could I do this to Zoe?

How could one mistake hurt so many people?

"Zoe. You're all I think about. I mean it. You're my motivation to come back home. I'm not blaming a substance, but this shit happens, and feelings can get inflated." I begged her to understand, "I know, it's no excuse."

"Exactly. You said it yourself. Drugs are no excuse." She sighed. "I need some time to work through this. Just don't contact me for a while. I'll reach out if I'm ready."

The *if* is what got me. I would have much preferred a *when*. We shared a genuine connection, and a reckless, senseless night like that should never have even been conceived. I wanted Zoe, and I couldn't help but feel a deserved massive guilt over doing something so selfishly irresponsible. It was one thing to be honest and confess it to her, which I do not regret because it was the right thing to do considering I could've easily lied about it, but it was another thing to engage with another woman at all. I didn't even have the chance to vent the datura experience to her. I knew I fucked up. She was the first female I'd had conversations with in relation to having children and growing old. I know we hadn't possessed anything materially concrete in terms of a physical relationship yet, but the spiritual connection between us meant more than that—some kind of unspoken bond, and I hoped to God that I hadn't just sabotaged it.

Johnny sat in front of me at the kitchen table and crossed his arms, sipping his coffee and exhausted from our elongated stay in Granada. As was I. He sighed. "I think it's time we left Europe."

Johnny's withdrawals seemed all but gone. I think this experience was able to wipe his addiction, but at what cost?

Chapter 12

THE FACE OF EXTREME PLEASURE

On the plane to the United States, Johnny and I were far too exhausted to even speak about what we went through. Peering through the round window on the flight, I could have sworn I caught the face of a child staring back at me in the clouds but it only lasted a second. I feared the flashbacks were appearing again—unless the crew had been infusing something funky into the aeroplane food.

I wish I could tell you what happened to Lagos. He later came up in conversation on the flight as Johnny jabbed his fork into his steamed carrots as if he hadn't eaten in months.

"He's probably dead. He woulda tripped outta his mind and fell off some cliff or trench to meet his peril, for sure." Johnny's speculation made me wonder how much of a 'friend' Lagos really was to him. He didn't seem concerned, or bothered over the fate of his Milanese mate.

The death would make sense, as nobody would find him for days and possibly weeks. Either way, the lack of communication from him would be expected regardless, considering the junkie in him. But after everything, we never saw, nor heard from Lagos ever again.

*

Johnny and I shared quite the lengthy discussion on which US state we were set to engage the air brakes on, but I think we both knew exactly where we'd end up, whether we were throwing other cities into the mix just for the sake of having options—it was always going to be Vegas.

Upon landing, we needed to ground ourselves—*literally*. I pulled out the list that we hadn't touched since Queensland, Australia, and decided to cross off whatever we'd achieved. After undergoing a dark moment in life—like Johnny battling a quick onset addiction or being attacked by a psycho on what was more than a heroic dose—perhaps a *demonic* dose—of an evil plant, the wise thing to do is stand back and look at your place in life, taking a second to breathe and gain a wider perspective before being sucked into the next void. Observing the list, adding a few items and crossing a few off, I noticed only two remained. We were surprised, wondering how in the hell we achieved that much and stayed on our feet, let alone *survived*. The only two drugs we hadn't ticked off yet was ether—an old school anaesthetic and an additive to jet fuel—and the last just happened to theoretically be the heaviest, most daunting substance of them all: *Ayahuasca.* But I had the feeling we'd get to that down in

Peru, where we'd planned to travel right away after Vegas.

The Neon City was a stop-off in between as a chance to get some rest, let our hair down and return to Earth before setting off in another country with a foreign language. The only problem was that in Vegas, you don't chase the drugs—*they chase you.*

I was able to get my hands on a small bottle of raw ether. Now, Johnny and I had this idea from a book we read which you may have heard of—*Fear and Loathing in Las Vegas by Hunter S. Thompson.* In the novel, ether was used as an inhalant that slows the messages from your brain to your gross motor skills, leaving you in a state of absolute uselessness—yet, you'd still be cognitively functional, simply watching your body behave in that uncontrollable manner. The reason we awaited the United States journey to try it was because Vegas feeds off fools. It's arguably the only place in the world where you could be shit-faced, out of your fucking mind or simply dragging yourself on the ground like the limbless undead—and still be allowed access to some establishments all because they know you'll be intoxicated enough to blow your life savings on a roll of the dice. You won't be the only one. Vegas is rampant with these people, so slurring your words, tripping over your heels and being as high as a Neptune-bound astronaut is the norm in this town, and nobody would bat an eye because they know where they are: *Sin City.*

*

Beer. I was never the biggest fan, aside from the occasional quench of thirst on a searing summer's day. Johnny had sunk three in a row between the airport and our apartment at the Fontainebleau. For me, beer is far too bloating, even the light stuff. I'd rather save room for more bourbon or gin. Also, it adds pounds to your stomach, not that general alcohol doesn't damage your body in other ways—still, I'd rather not have what they'd call a 'beer belly'.

At our new apartment with only a bed and a minibar, Johnny cracked opened his fourth when I suggested he cool his jets a little.

"We're about to get into an ether binge," I warned. "Slow down because it'll only make it worse."

I probably should've left him to it. In hindsight, he was likely using the beer as a means to get over his run-in with ice. I should've encouraged it if anything.

"We've got the entire day. I gotta keep the spirits up somehow," Johnny protested, chugging his ale of hops and barley.

I never really considered it until later, but these little sentences Johnny would say was quite indicative that he had an addictive personality. As much as we had a swelling curiosity about worldwide drugs, Johnny and I were two very different people, and these drugs affected us in many ways. He gained dependence on them with little resistance. As for me, I'd always had a yearning to try good drugs again, but never had I abused them, or sought them out for pure satisfaction. What I noticed a long time ago—and I think it's an important piece of information—is for some that like smoking cigarettes, shall *smoke* that cigarette. We humans should always do and try things that make us happy—*whatever that word really mean*s—but not to abuse them and never to depend on them, especially when your body asks for it.

If you smoke a cigarette for the first time out of curiosity, it's fine. If you're out, having fun and your friend offers you another, *it's quite all right*. But if you're home alone, and feel the need for a cigarette, that's when you resist. Stay the fuck away from it and don't purchase that packet—because that's how dependency begins. With you giving your body what it's asking for and feeding its craving. That's how these addictions sustain themselves. It's not about the action of doing it—but seeking it out and satisfying your brain's request is where the mistake is made. This goes for every drug, any alcohol and generally anything addictive. Yes, that includes chewing fingernails, scrolling the internet and gambling.

*

Johnny and I arrived at the tables, although we couldn't place many bets due to having limited funds in our accounts. We'd still planned to see South America before heading back home and couldn't afford to splurge.

The time ticked past 11p.m. which for us, was ether o'clock. Still plenty early, but late enough to make a few mistakes and steer clear of the family frenzies. To participate in this wild sport, we required a cloth of some kind but with the lack of clothes we'd packed—some being torn and soiled during the datura fiasco, and some even being stolen in Ottakring—we were only left with two pairs of underwear. We'd been wearing the same clothes for about a week. In the bathroom, we occupied a stall.

"They better not catch us," Johnny whispered as I pulled the underwear out of my pocket. *Don't fret*—it was a squeaky-clean pair, freshly washed.

"Which part?" I said, opening the bottle and soaking the tighty-whities with it. "Huffing raw ether, or sniffing a pair of men's underwear in a bathroom?"

Johnny cracked up. It was the first time I'd seen those facial muscles contract since Amsterdam. Being caught committing either act would result in our immediate ejection from the premises. You'd be out of there before you could even feel the high—which comes on pretty quick. I'd still prefer to be booted out for inhaling junk than looking like some creep sniffing undergarments.

"How 'bout a napkin?" I suggested.

"It'll fall apart after two huffs." Johnny shook his head. "And we'll keep wasting the liquid on new napkins."

Ether is almost paralysing. I was never one for taking substances for purposes they weren't originally meant for, but I was already neck-deep in this journey, which had seen me break that rule multiple times ... *so, why stop now?*

I allowed Johnny the first huff and he seemed moderately okay—a little lightheaded at first. I applied the same dose, huffing in a short, intense inhale. *Instant drunkenness.* I remember smiling, stupefied at the speed I was sent to the state of being wasted. Johnny followed shortly. Our voices fluctuated in highs and lows, as if a child were messing with a record player, jerking obsessively with the pitch control.

"Hoooo-oooly fucking ... *shit*." Johnny stared at the ceiling, dazed. I snatched the underwear for another huff to keep the experience consistent before Johnny fumbled the bottle.

Being glass, it shattered. The pungent smell of sweet, jet-fuel diethyl ether bombed out the bathroom. I stumbled in panic, half trying to escape the overwhelming, intoxicating smell to leave the room without being caught, while also trying to save the bottle that had already shattered.

"Shittt-t-t-t-t." Johnny's vocals were stretched. Then something strange happened. "Yo-ou fuckin' d-d-dropped it!" he stuttered, barely capable of expelling a syllable. "Nooo, na-na-na-no—" Johnny was glitching, repeating the same sound over and over, like a character in a poorly programmed videogame. "Na-na-na-na-na—" *Or was it me?*

It seemed like he was stuck in some stuttering loop. I tried to look away but my vision was greatly delayed, so unbelievably delayed that I could feel the cubicle wall with my hand before my vision could record my fingers touching it. *Fuck*, I thought, *it's not Johnny glitching, it's me*. My auditory senses were as if submerged, only picking up on the rushing liquids inside my brain. I then realised again that the ether bottle had been spilt and found myself kneeling, holding myself up on the door of the stall, trying to soak up as much liquid from the tiles as possible. And trust me, a Vegas bathroom on the ground floor of a building is never, ever clean.

Johnny leaned back against the wall of the stall with his mouth opened, and he closed his eyes. He was having some kind of trip. "Shut up! Who's in there?" Johnny screamed.

Nobody was in the bathroom with us. At least, I wasn't aware if they had been. I placed the soaked garment in my pocket and walked *casually* out of the stall, not being able to stop my body as it stumbled helplessly towards the sink. I was more than wasted—hammered, more than hammered—plastered, beyond control of my own limbs. It was as if some animal had possessed my body and was trying desperately to learn how to control the vessel of a human being—and I was only watching as a mere spectator.

"Daa-Johnny! Yourrralright?" I slurred, wondering if he could understand me, and paranoid that I was speaking too loudly.

I turned back around and looked at the open stall, but Johnny hadn't come out yet. The door to the bathrooms opened and I tried to act natural—*as natural as I could possibly act*. A man in a Hawaiian shirt strolled in with a fistful of cash, shoving it in his back pocket and looking at me somewhat peculiarly.

"What the hell is that smell?" he said with a highly prominent lisp. He walked towards the stall. "You fucken junkie." As he entered the stall, I'd forgotten somebody was in there. "Arrrgh!" he yelped.

The Hawaiian shirt guy almost fell to the ground, pulling away from an unsuspecting Johnny lurking in the stall. The man had also slipped upon the ether residue on the floor and scrambled away in his soaked cargo pants.

"*You* are what's wrong with America." He pointed at me. I tried to apologise but I could only speak in slurs. As he swung open the door, he turned around and pointed. "I'm calling security."

I spoke in his general direction. "You ... and what army?" It was as if somebody vaporised eight bottles of whisky and made me inhale the whole thing in one toke. By that time, he'd already fled the scene.

I opened the cubicle door to retrieve Johnny but after about thirty seconds of trying to get my body to reach the stall, I noticed the underwear, square over his face, soaking the ether directly into his nose, mouth and of course—his bloodstream. I thought it was in my pocket the whole time—*I must've imagined it.* I slapped it off his face before tumbling onto the toilet, sitting and letting my brain slow down for a second—even slower than it already was. Johnny just stood there. I expected some kind of psychosis after huffing that much. I expected to be attacked or to have Johnny rip off his clothes and sprint through the casino like a crazed lunatic, to then be kicked out for indecent exposure. But he just stood there and raised his hand slowly to the air in front of him, as if he were trying to reach for some kind of molecule suspended in thin air. *Beautiful in its way.* It was somewhat surreal to me, watching him reach for something that wasn't there in such momentary tranquillity. Maybe it was the ether, but it was a moment of complete purity. Johnny slowly extended his grasp for a non-existent object—right in front of my very eyes. His pupils, restricted to the width of a hand before him.

The next thing I remember is aggravated yelling, then being violently carried by someone. I couldn't see their faces, but I could only remember the carpet patterns on the floor, swaying side to side as if somebody had been dragging me, gripping me from the back of my shirt. We ended up outside the casino as the drug began to wear off—very quickly, I might add. Johnny still hadn't recovered. He just sat against a wall and gawked at all the cars passing by. I sat beside him and exhaled, letting the rest of the ether wear off. In the back of my mind, I wondered if Johnny was broken, as if all that ether had soaked into his brain, sterilising it or something. But that thought was a frequent one. I'd had far too many moments worrying whether Johnny would recover from these heavy trips—he'd always return to Earth eventually.

Johnny finally sobered up after a few minutes, looked at me and smiled. "Fucken ether." We sat there for about an hour, just taking in the surroundings.

A peculiar detail I noticed about the ether was that it may *not* have been raw diethyl ether. After replacing it as an anaesthetic in the 1960s, the US now only utilises its properties as a solvent for the manufacture of dyes and plastics. The reason I question the purity was due to the odd, uncharacteristic auditory distortion and repetition I was experiencing in the cubicle. I would've checked the bottle for additional additives, but it was left shattered on the bathroom floor and I couldn't remember the brand of it. *Or, maybe I'm overthinking it?* Maybe I underestimated the power of ether.

Johnny explained the bathroom experience to be excessively psychedelic and overwhelming, hearing voices yelling at him and pounding on the cubicle wall. He even recalled a colourful monster barging into the stall—which from my perspective was simply the guy in the Hawaiian shirt. He then said he saw a substance in thin air, a real singularity. *Some kind of orb.* He tried to reach for it, grab it. The trip was persuading him, urging him to consume it, but he simply couldn't reach it. His vision also played up after soaking the underwear into his face. He told me that he could move the Earth with his mind. Everywhere he looked, the tiles on the floor changed shape and followed according to his eye movements. The door in front of him wobbled open and closed at an incomprehensible speed. He even looked at me when I'd sat down beneath him on the toilet seat. He turned me into spaghetti with his eyes, swirling me and morphing me into some artistic Salvador Dali piece. He clearly reached another level of this trip.

November 11th

The shadows beneath Johnny's eyes were clearing up and he was already looking healthier in complexion. This was due to his replenished appetite and daily intake of essential nutrients but most importantly, sufficient sleep. It's amazing how quickly one can regain their health, and how quickly one can deteriorate.

Three updates to the journal took place in Vegas. The aforementioned was one of them. The next one was a little more mellow, but can be excruciatingly addictive. *Morphine.* As many know, morphine is used to relieve severe pain. I seemed to be breaking a few of the same rules in this city regarding the trial of substances in a recreational manner. After a few nights, Johnny met a couple of acquaintances at the bar and they gave him two syrettes to try for ourselves. I've never injected anything into my body before, but Johnny claimed they swore by it.

"If we're documenting a journal centred around the use of drugs, we should have every method of administration down pat," Johnny reasoned—a weak justification for intravenous injection.

Along with rectal administration—the idea of jabbing myself disgusted me. Another factor that frightened me is that morphine is one of the four 'end of life' drugs. These drugs are used to sedate people, block dopamine receptors, halt seizures and regulate bladder movements when somebody is on the path to the tunnel of light. Nevertheless, Johnny purchased these syrettes and elected to ride them out in a safe environment. For me, that meant our hotel room. For Johnny, it meant a movie theatre.

Morphine is not a party drug, and it's not a psychedelic. It's opium, one of the most highly pleasurable, tremendously addictive substances ever to exist on God's green Earth. Heroin is basically morphine—but on a much heavier, addictive and dangerous scale. I was happy to stay away from it, but morphine was simply not so much safer. In this day and age, we simply could have taken morphine as a pill, or even smoked it. But Johnny happened to come by syrettes and decided that it'd be a welcomed addition to the works.

I wasn't in any position to disagree.

We booked two tickets to an old theatre nearby and decided it was best to see something with minimal public interest. That either meant an indie film, or a documentary. Our minds were made up when we noticed a midnight screening of an ocean documentary, narrated by none other than David Attenborough.

Johnny and I sat parallel in the centre seats of the empty theatre, taking deep breaths and entering a relaxed state prior to injection. I used this moment as a chance to fill Johnny in on the Erin and Zoe situation. He kept asking about Zoe and how it was going with her. I couldn't keep him in the dark much longer.

"Dude, that's heavy." Johnny was surprised at my actions, knowing I'd had better judgement in the past. "If it makes ya feel any better, there's a chance Erin would've cheated on her husband regardless. It just happened to be with you."

"That might ease my mind on the Erin front, but it doesn't fix the Zoe situation."

There wasn't much more I could say on the matter. I thought about messaging her, just to check in, but decided against it.

Morphine was easily one of the drugs that I felt regret over choosing to take. The funny thing is, it's probably the least harmful at its peak—you're just sitting there feeling fantastically fucking terrific—but administering it through the vein feels absolutely wrong, and this kind of usage belongs either in a hospital—or with cold, hard junkies, riddled with withdrawal and on the verge of death.

Upon finding a vein and injecting a syrette each, Johnny smiled after about three seconds. "I can feel it already. It's cold." We'd both never had the experience of a drug take hold that quickly. The only things to come close were salvia and ether.

Morphine travels through the bloodstream and attaches itself to the opioid receptors in the brain. *There is no quicker way to get high.* I felt my body numb itself, piece by piece, limb by limb, resting our legs on the row in front of us. At that point, I gazed far ahead of myself and came to a sudden realisation. *Johnny's feet are so much bigger than mine.* I laughed at the random thought and closed my eyes. The muscles in my neck completely relaxed and I felt intensely pleasurable nerves trickling up and down my muscles. All the cells in my body felt as if submerged in a warm bath. The seahorse gliding along the coral reef on the big screen seemed to only enhance the experience of grace and sublimity.

Johnny scrunched his sweater over his face. "Jesus Christ, it's like an internal orgasm in my bloodstream." At that point, I heard someone get up from the rows behind and speedily exit the theatre. We assumed we were alone. I guess they must've thought we were having some extraordinarily spectacular sex to the luscious backdrop of a sea documentary.

Every time I took a breath, I'd feel my back sinking into the seat beneath me, but the rest of my body was quite the contrary. A floating sensation, a feeling of levitation embraced me, so strong that I felt I could touch the ceiling. I had to grip the armrests to remind myself that I was still grounded. I turned to Johnny, and with the projected blue colours shimmering over his face, he looked to have found complete nirvana in his dose. He was just sitting there, smiling. That's all, just smiling. People say it's one of the most dangerous drugs, but the drug itself isn't all that bad—it's the drive to achieve that rewarding feeling again, and again. Gaining a tolerance is one of the genuine factors to blame for this. Every time you take morphine or heroin, the effects lessen as your body builds a tolerance—so you need more and more every time to feel that same sensation over and over again—and every time you're sober, the world isn't as colourful as you remember it—you simply want to feel happy again, as happy as you did on morphine.

*

After what was, without doubt, the most straightforward experience we'd had so far, we decided to return to the party scene. After all, it was Las Vegas. We were relaxing poolside on the morning after the morphine session. Johnny fell victim to a fever at dawn and wanted to get out into the sun. Chills and goose bumps are a common side effect after the use of opioids, so this was somewhat expected. There were other bathers in the vicinity of the hotel pool, but nobody was swimming. It was one of those days where the ultraviolet rays felt nice on the skin, but the water wasn't quite warm enough to tread.

Johnny stirred his vodka orange with a straw and stared into the sky with his shades on. "Remember that bar a few nights back?"

I nodded, kicking my feet up and soaking in the cool Nevada sun. "Yeah, when that douche spilt his drink on me and didn't apologise?"

"That's the one." Johnny sipped his drink as a waiter brought me another.

"What about it?"

"Remember that guy, Steve?" Johnny asked. "The one with the lawnmowed haircut?"

I crossed my arms, "He was going on about that fat DJ in town, yes?"

"He mentioned something called Meow when you were in the bathroom." Johnny grinned.

I sat up and removed my shades. "When the hell were you gonna tell me about this? What the fuck is Meow?"

"I just didn't think you were keen on it until I had a thought last night." Johnny sat up too. "For the last few months, you've mainly been seeking psychedelics but after the ether, and after the morphine, it sounds like you're still up for a funky time regardless. It's a dissociative-empathogen."

I stared at Johnny, hesitant. "Well, first we gotta find out what the fuck Meow is and if it's worth fucking with."

Johnny sighed and removed his shades. "It's not the drug that's the problem. It's how we're gonna acquire it."

Mephedrone. *A new-world drug.* A younger substance to the market, also known as Meph, Meow, M-Cat, Bubbles and Kitty Cat. I'm sure you can tell by now that these nicknames were by no means crafted by literary geniuses. Originally marketed as a plant fertiliser or a research chemical—like any drug—teenagers soon discovered that it gives you a scorching high, especially in a club around people, and *especially* around some killer tunes.

After all the psychedelics we'd taken, all the stimulants, depressants, opioids and dissociatives, it was time to get back into the rush of an empathogen. Although compared to Kitty Cat, MDMA is considered safe ... Mephedrone is basically molly mixed with ketamine. As much as this scared us, it excited us for the next, and quite possibly the last, party drug we'd take on this trip. All we had to do was get our hands on it, and Johnny's new friends told us just how to obtain it.

The crack side of town was where all the meth-heads and dodgy dealers would swarm and wander the streets. You had a forty percent chance of coming across a junkie, asking if you knew where the hook-up was. You had a thirty-five percent chance of some hooker with missing teeth offering you a gummy blowjob for twenty bucks. And you had a twenty-five percent chance of being mugged.

We roamed the midnight streets to a boarded-up house, but it looked more like an old diner. I looked at Johnny, tugging on his arm, "Maybe this isn't a good idea, dude."

He shrugged. "Jean's literally waiting for us inside. This is the address, man."

I studied the place and the neighbourhood surrounding us. I still wasn't convinced. "Dude, this is the first time we've actually gone out of our way to purchase anything illegal without obtaining it naturally or through someone in a safe space."

Johnny didn't seem to pick up what I was putting down. "You're overreacting. Wanna have a good time tonight, or what?"

"Not if I'm going to die before it happens." I stopped.

Johnny placed his hand on my shoulder. "Just trust me—this guy said he's cool."

I couldn't deter him, so I stopped trying, especially if it meant additional content for my journalism. I should've said no. I should've just walked away.

Slowly stepping into the building, I had a worrisome aura overcome my body. I even began to sweat. Situations like these are super tense. You act slightly suspicious, and you'll be shot or stabbed in a heartbeat. It was almost as if we were walking through an old diner in some post-apocalyptic videogame.

"We should get a little extra. Maybe even a second baggie. We could sell it or use it for next time," Johnny whispered as we tiptoed through the eerie hallway.

I'd had my doubts the entire time about Johnny, but this was the kicker—he seemed to have lost grasp of what we were doing here, and what the intention of this documentation was. And he deliberately mentioned it inside a quiet space so I couldn't voice heavy protest. We'd set rules that he no longer felt the need to abide. All these drugs should only be done once in this study, if not avoided altogether. Mephedrone is dangerous, and I didn't understand why he wanted to purchase more for later. I think maybe he wanted to feel like risking his life for a drug was worthwhile, rather than almost being shot over a single baggie that'd last only three to six hours.

We were welcomed by a friendly face, Ian. "You two from town?"

He had unusually large ears and a major receding hairline. He reminded me of that little bald guy—Schlitzie from *Freaks*.

"Yeah, Jean sent us." Johnny gulped. I could tell he was feeling the spiders crawl up his spine.

"*Jean?* I don't know any Jean." Ian's piercing eyes were impaling Johnny's, fooling us into the fear that we'd strolled into some kind of trap. Ian sniggered. "I'm fucking with you. How many grams did he say?"

Sweet relief, but we weren't out of the woods yet. Johnny tried to avoid eye contact. "He didn't. We were hoping for two baggies." Making eye contact could be seen as a threat to an unstable human being, so it's best not to challenge the alpha in his domain.

He walked us to a backroom where he said he kept the 'stuff'. It was a lot sketchier than anything we'd encountered before. The smell of toxins and potent chemicals poisoned the air, accompanied by stained walls, unidentified spills and a beaten-up dog kennel with no signs of a canine. Up until this point, the only thing scaring us was our anxieties, until Ian showed us the 'stuff'. It was a lot more yellowish than expected. As I worried, Johnny seemed to believe it was adequate, or at least tried to convince himself that it was. I decided to let him purchase one bag, rather than cause a fuss and let this guy expose his product and turn him down. All sorts of crap could be unleashed, especially with an unpredictable meth-head in a possible meth *lab*.

Upon acquiring the bag, which we paid a hundred and eighteen bucks for, Ian mentioned that he had a cache of crystal. Johnny's eyes lit up as if NYE and the fourth of July were on the same day. I knew he'd been craving it. Cutting an addiction doesn't mean stopping for a few weeks or a few months. If you continue using, even after a while, then you never really recovered. Cutting an addiction means you never do it ever again—*ever*. Johnny knew I wouldn't have a bar of it if he thought about purchasing a baggie of meth from Ian, so he contained himself.

Leaving unscathed, I glanced at the bag again. I had never seen white powder look so yellow before. Johnny was so hell bent on trying it that he was willing to overlook a red flag like this; however, the ignorance of any abnormality could be horrifically consequential when it comes to any drug.

We finally stepped out of the shoddy house before being immediately approached by some skinny junkie hooker with jittery nerves. She had the *meth-face* and a few bald spots. "Whatcha pick up? A lil baggy?" She'd clearly been lurking outside, lip-licking and fiendishly obsessing over the product within.

Johnny snatched the bag to himself, close to his heart. It seemed more important than his own life.

"My name's Elnie. Just lookin' for a bump. You got some?" She jabbed at Johnny repeatedly. But as far gone as he was, he'd never hit or take a swing at any female— junkie or not. She laughed, trying to grab the bag off him. "Just a bump, c'mon just a bump, Hot Stuff. I'll give you the private show." She felt up her own scraggly body in a failed attempt of seduction.

I couldn't help but cringe, wondering what her version of a private show was, considering the condition of her hair, teeth, skin and nails. Johnny turned around quickly. "Just fuck off, all right?"

People tend to like you and treat you kindly when they think they can get something out of you. In fact, it's not just this town—*people are like this everywhere.* They keep a smile on their face, the polite words in their mouth and act like you're a dear friend of theirs—*until you're not.* Elnie's face completely switched, as if another being possessed her consciousness. She gave Johnny a sour look as if he'd just bashed her three times in the face—but to be fair, she'd already looked that way prior.

"Tell me to fuck off? Who the fuck are you? Gimme that bag! You know who I know? I can get you killed out here. Gimme dat fuckin' bag!" She latched on to Johnny, and he began squirming as if she was a starved, demonic, hairless house cat. Other hooded figures began emerging from behind buildings in the distance after overhearing the fuss. This was getting dangerous.

Elnie scratched Johnny a few times, which worried me because she drew blood from his forearm and whatever diseases or viruses she had could've been transmitted to Johnny. I was concerned that he'd wake up a zombie the next day. Johnny shook her off to the ground. I'm pretty sure I heard her spine crack a little on the pavement. She didn't care, especially when there was an opportunity to get a sniff. For people like this, one bump is worth months of dangling around the poles on the street corners of Cracktown.

Johnny turned around to walk away with me, but it wasn't over. This bitch came right back, harder than ever.

She headbutted Johnny in the spine and he fell to the ground. We needed to hurry, or we'd risk our entire night and possibly our whole Vegas trip dealing with this relentless creature. Her eyes were like that of a Great White, black and soulless, approaching Johnny, licking her lips, salivating at the thought of the white-yellow powder entering her bloodstream.

"Just give her the fucking bag!" I urged him. "She's just gonna keep following us. It's not worth it, Johnny!"

Johnny shook his head, scooting away from her. She stepped even closer, threatening to launch at any second. She was ready to tear out his oesophagus for a mere quarter-gram.

"Gimme da fuckin' bag, you cocksucker." She intensely pointed. "Gimme dat bag!"

She sprung, latching on to Johnny, attempting to rip the bag from his grasp. Instead, it popped. The thin dust rained over the three of us and Elnie screeched as if we mutilated her only child in front of her very eyes. She immediately kneeled to the ground and vacuumed any dust she could cram into her nostrils with wide eyes, but most of it was already swept up into the desert air and a part of Nevada along with all the other drugs in this town. Johnny and I walked away while she snorted along the pavement like a hound looking for a place to shit.

"Fuck!" Johnny stomped as we headed towards the nearest public place for safety. "I just wanted to get a taste, man."

"They obviously know there's a dealer there, so the junkies wait outside that joint." I sighed. Johnny shook his head. I've never seen him so disappointed over a drug before. "Look, it was probably for the best ..." I consoled.

"... considering how yellow that powder was, and we avoided a potentially homicidal hooker."

*

The next morning, I woke up to a hellish hangover. After our lack of access to the product, which may have been a good thing, we turned to trusty alcohol for our night on the town. I always tell myself to remember to drink water but when I'm intoxicated, there seems to be no such substance as H2O, and all you want is additional drinks. I woke up alone because Johnny booked another apartment for the two girls he'd brought back to bed. Maybe he wanted to make it up to himself and feel like his craving for substances was somewhat satisfied. Our flight to Peru was prebooked and we were set to leave at 7:34 p.m. I packed everything, ventured downstairs for an overpriced short black and woke myself up before blowing eighty bucks on red. I considered messaging Zoe to deconstruct the ordeal from the night before, but thought better of it. If she were to forgive me, the least I could do was abide by her rules and wait for her to contact *me*.

By 1 p.m., there was still no sign of Johnny. Either his headache was too grisly and needed most of the day to rest, or he was spending the day with those girls.

By 4:30 p.m. I became a little concerned over Johnny's whereabouts. Even the fucked-up Europe-Johnny would remember that we had a flight. I kept faith, hoping he'd show up at any second, even after none of my phone calls had been answered or returned.

It was 6 p.m. and I went to his apartment, knocked on it and found it was unlocked. It was empty. Although, it smelt like sex. The sweat, the sourness, the bras, underwear and bottles of empty lube proved that he'd had a busy night. I stepped into the bathroom, searching for any sign of his whereabouts with just over an hour until our flight was due to depart. Three more bras were on the bathroom floor. My guess would be that the two girls he brought back had friends they invited to the apartment. At this point, you'd believe he was humped to death by a gang of savage Vegas women.

By 7:15 p.m. I was at the airport, hoping Johnny would show up in the nick of time like some sappy romantic drama. Maybe his phone died, and he couldn't find me. I remained hopeful, clinging to the possibility that he'd explain everything when he arrived. If he didn't show up, I had a serious decision to make: either go back into town and seek him out, or ditch the fucker for Peru. I needed to continue my journey, especially if it meant getting back to Zoe and straightening things out. After some thought, I realised I couldn't do that to him. I was ready to head back into town.

Minutes before the flight, I received his text:

JOHNNY:

'Take the plane without me. Found some cool friends here. Not ready to leave just yet.'

Chapter 13

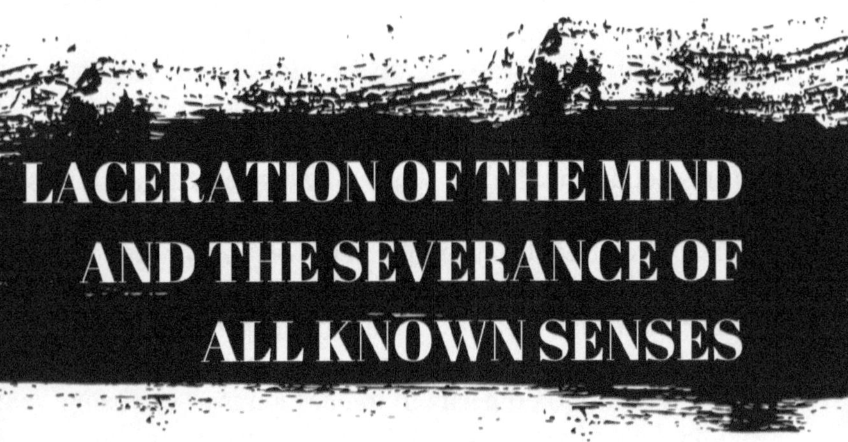

Ayahuasca will either be the most frightening thing you'll ever do, or the most enlightening thing you've ever done. Mindset is the real judge of which it'd be. Setting is another factor—but being with a shaman in a traditional ritual assists in preventing a bad experience and unlocks a truly sacred event. The only other thing that can affect this trip is luck. You will change forever after smoking, drinking or ingesting this drug in any way, potentially more so than all the others—and the effects last far, far longer. Huasca is more closely related to medicine as opposed to being a recreational 'drug'. Cultures and ancient societies have been brewing it in ceremonies for thousands of years to purge evil, illness and negativity from the body, including trauma and grief.

I had to board the plane to Peru after I received Johnny's text. If he was in potential trouble, I would have held back but since he was staying in Vegas for purely recreational purposes—*or so he claimed*—I had no choice but to continue my journey and finish what I'd begun. I had no more time to waste, and no more money left to spend. Truthfully, I was a little concerned over my financial state upon arrival back home but that was an issue I preferred to encounter later on. This wasn't a journey of journalism anymore—it had become much more than that to me. After the experiences with mescaline, salvia—maybe even datura—and some of the other substances, I'd been left to question my very being and the idea of who I was and what my imminent future held in store for me. I don't think anyone truly knows who they are, but with the influence of these substances and the seeds they planted in my brain, it sent me on a pathway of curiosity and self-wonder, things I hadn't even considered delving into before. The more time I spent alone, from Amsterdam to Grenada to Nevada, the more I pondered these screaming thoughts inside my head—a yearning to explore my inner eye.

November 24th

I caught a bus from a crammed airport to an ayahuasca retreat, where they perform group ceremonies ranging from about eight to sixteen people. Initially, I didn't want my journal involving the influence or experience of random other people, especially if it meant vomiting or defecating in front of them which is a common instance during this potentially brain-splitting experience I was soon to swan dive into. Unfortunately, there wasn't an option to do this alone; at least, not at *this* retreat. It was a well-renowned venue with apparent higher potency in brew. I was soon reassured by the shaman, a thirty-nine-year-old woman with braided hair. Her highlighting feature was her sincere, genuine smile. You could tell she'd participated in these ceremonies many times herself. The smile would almost distract you from the strangulation marks around her neck. Indications of past physical and likely, mental trauma.

Her English was more fluent than the other shamans. I assumed they utilised her to speak to foreigners. "Other participants won't have any influence on your experience. If they ever do, it usually has a positive impact on yours." She smiled and nodded, "We're *all* one here."

I felt a little like a stranger, like a fraud, taking part in a ritualistic cult under a religion that I knew nothing about. What kept me there was the fact that there were many others just like me, foreigners to Peru. I wondered if they also felt like imposters, some in ripped jeans, some in crop tops, exploiting a medicine prepared by, and for, another culture. Johnny wasn't there for this one. This was the last drug on the list, and probably the most anticipated by calibre. I wasn't in it for the rush, or the high, or the thrill. I wanted to extract as much information from my brain as possible, find some kind of enlightenment, and maybe get some answers about myself, who I am and what the purpose of my life is. I wanted to have positive takeaways—the ability to connect more with others, more empathy, more kindness and contentment, worry less about how others perceive me, so I could be my true self without judgement. Maybe the reason I set upon this journey in the first place was because I didn't know what the fuck I wanted out of life. Maybe that's what I'd been searching for. I wanted to be awake and understand better the world around me. Even if it meant exploring my deepest and darkest fears, anxieties and memories.

I looked over at the man beside me, about sixty with a long white beard, lying sideways and rocking himself back and forth. He looked at me. "They can't control the creatures in your mind, but they have the key to open the gate."

Before trying ayahuasca, you should have a good idea about what your motives are—as I've mentioned before, this is not a thrill-seeking drug, no real psychedelic is. If that's what you're looking for, stick to ketamine or MDMA on a low dose. Psychedelics are drugs that require respect—*I cannot stress that enough.* In fact, it feels wrong to even refer to these psychedelics as drugs anymore. They're almost tools, spiritual compounds that allow you to explore your most inner self on another spectrum of consciousness. Being in the same category as cocaine, ice, alcohol and prescription pills is an insult to these substances and the benefits they have to offer.

Johnny and I set off on this journey with the intent of trying and documenting every drug we could get our hands on. If we'd simply followed the basic guideline, I wouldn't have had the respect, nor the right to try ayahuasca. After the few real psychedelic experiences, I had opened my mind to believe that there's far more than just what we see. Something metaphysical. A specific thought that had stuck with me from these experiences is a simple fact: *Nothing would exist without the abilities to detect them.* Our senses are but a window into our waking universe. Taking these otherworldly substances is a full-blown view into our psyche and what we are beyond the material plane. I don't expect the inexperienced to fully comprehend it, but this is *my* experience with it—and collectively, many others'.

I had this overwhelming feeling that this was part of my master plan. I realised I wasn't just some naive journalist who wanted to document as many chemicals as he could cram into his veins. The universe sent me on this journey to explore these hidden worlds and understand my inner workings. *A complete sense of humbling in the almightiest way.* I was supposed to come up with the idea through journalism so it could send me to this exact point in my life. Thinking about God isn't how I used to think God was—he is not a single entity; he is not a single man up in the clouds. God is collectively the *entire universe* in everything we see and everything we do. My conclusion is that these substances have been placed on Earth naturally to allow us humans to experience a higher state of mind and promote discovery of what the universe really is—a window into what is actually going on, whether I'm referring to the world itself, or the happenings inside your brain. These substances are built to expand us in ways that no mere inexperienced human can ever comprehend. I'm not saying that the giant mantis you see on a mescaline trip is real and that it's your true god, but the perception of them, the idea of them and the messages they pass on to you can be as real as your material vessel. Even the most ridiculous, hilariously amusing trips can turn out to have some kind of important underlying message.

*

I sat down with a more experienced shaman, another woman. They were used to foreigners who wanted this experience without having to speak Spanish. The way they'd communicate was very simple and quite easy to understand by basically pointing at something, conveying an emotion or gesture, like pretending to drink a cup meant to sip the tea. It was a very primal version of sign language and the easiest way to understand someone without having to use a specific language. I sat down with a shaman after paying her two hundred and fifty dollars. The entire camp was quite small and there were about twelve others in the enormous tent. The shaman—a regular-looking Peruvian woman (I expected most of them to look almost primal, with painted skin and bone necklaces of sorts) smiled at me with a nod. It was almost as if she were reassuring me, understanding my lack of belonging. This encouraged me to feel welcomed and involved. *One ounce of kindness could change everything.*

Prior to these ceremonies, it's imperative that you avoid red meat, spicy food and sex. Most of which was quite easy for me. The shaman left for a minute and I controlled my breaths, taking in the sounds of nature surrounding us and following a calm pattern of inhales and exhales. She returned with the pot of brewed tea, signalling for everyone to stand up slowly and take a shot-sized cup, drink it down and relax for about an hour before doing it again. The two shamans handed out toilet paper rolls, buckets and grapes to everyone in the large, spacious circle.

I began to see little blue, red and green dots moving around me, consuming the entire room. The shaman's face blurred. I felt the bitter taste of the extract reach my stomach much later than expected. It started with intense hot flushes and sweat. Within that hour, I'd already begun seeing reality rip itself apart and force me into the body of a snake among the Amazon, as if the plant itself was showing me what *it* had witnessed as part of the Earth. This thought connected with my confronting experience with salvia, as if the two went hand in hand. I wasn't seeing life go by as a tree or an animal, I was *feeling* it. I'd felt the pain of the Earth and all the universe's suffering go right through me from biblical times to ancient, to modern and every single singularity and piece of the Earth, everyone within it and every speck of the universe pass through my soul. After slipping into the water as the snake, feeling the dirt beneath me become sand, I glanced up at the ceiling of the tent. The shaman passed me another cup of the tea. I was in sweats before throwing up.

Thankfully, I hadn't defecated yet. The taste was unbearable—possibly the most foul-tasting liquid I had ever consumed. It felt as if I was swallowing my own pain and innermost emotions in a single cup, purging them out into that bucket. The sweats triggered negativity as I began to hyperventilate. I needed to calm down—*calm the fuck down.* This wasn't the time to freak out or quit. When you're taking part in an ayahuasca ritual, you're either all in, or you don't do it at all.

During these thoughts, I'd actually forgotten about the last sip and was sent into a trip like a bus hitting me at the speed of a jet plane. At first, all my senses disappeared. I couldn't see, hear, smell, taste or feel. I was but a floating consciousness in space that felt like the time before Earth had even been conceived. There was no such thing as time—it was only emptiness, endless and vast space where I yet again had the similar feeling to salvia, the fear that I'd be here forever, and I'd never leave. Then that fear became acceptance—and then power, as I felt the nothingness around me sway up and down like nerves, except I had no body. I thought my sense of feeling was returning—even though in that space and time, the concept of feeling anything, being alive or even living my life or any idea who I am or what matter is, was utterly incomprehensible. I realised that movement in general was based entirely on my heartbeat. The world, the universe and everything in between was moving to the beat of my own heart. I'd been controlling it and it had been happening during and before my existence. The faster I allowed my heart to beat, the quicker things seemed to move, not time—in this strange place there was no such thing as time, no such concept, but these lights and particles were moving with my heart. Then something changed. I slowed my heart rate dramatically—somehow voluntarily with ease. These pieces of light reduced speed almost to a stop. At the time, I worried that if they came to a complete stop, the world would end, and it'd be all my fault.

An orb of light seemed to slow down just enough for me to look into it, before being sucked entirely into its void. I heard the voice of the man sitting next to me again, except it wasn't his voice. It can be better explained as a feeling. "They can't control the creatures in your mind, but they have the key to open the gate."

I was met instantly by some kind of fucked-up, hairy, mutated creature with four noses on its face and giant claws. I had the overwhelming feeling that it wasn't some random depiction of a beast that my creative brain had orchestrated—it was all my negative thoughts, opinions, emotions, memories, traumatic experiences and wrongdoings that had manifested into some grotesque beast inside me, raging to get out. In my brain—or wherever my conscience was at the time—I believed that it was the literal entity that showed itself every time I'd been a bad person, a bad friend, made a bad decision or had simply birthed a negative thought. I was reintroduced to the fact that I was a being, with all my senses absorbed back into me in dramatic fashion. It was my own life from an outer perspective, yet more introspective than anything—as if I'd ripped open the brain of the being where my consciousness resided, to scoop out and analyse the interior. This frightening beast was physical, existing inside me, and it had always been there, even before I had existed, waiting for me—assigned to me. I concluded that everybody has this beast, even if these beasts might look different and speak without speaking. This whole experience so far made me feel like I'd been injected with an abundance of information and intelligence, as if the Earth was explaining to me how fragile it is and how important every single person is within it. I returned to the beast inside me and realised that I wasn't supposed to battle with it or kill it. I had this unquestionable insight about how the world needs balance—the yin yang sort of mentality. A balance of good and evil, positive and negative, sinfulness and righteousness. I wasn't supposed to fight tooth and nail with this beast—I was meant to accept it. And it would be forever a part of me. I wasn't supposed to defeat it, nor let it take over my consciousness but more so control it and let it live within me, even if it doesn't show itself in my reality. This creature is a prerequisite to being a human, but our job is to keep it in its cage.

I woke up again, never really having fallen asleep and the shaman was singing, lightly tapping a small drum with her eyes closed. I felt the need to throw up but was able to keep it down. She noticed I was awake and poured me another cup—*one more*. I knew I must continue, as mentally and physically exhausted as I was, and as much as I wanted to self-debrief over what just happened—it was part of my journey. I knew I needed to go the full distance. Little did I know that this would be the most powerful part of the experience yet—I proceeded to drink it down.

This time I didn't even get a chance to recall falling into it, or even closing my eyes. The pictures I saw were almost as if my sight were a TV screen with fuzz and sudden fluctuations in frequency. I understood this to be the segment before time, before God, before the universe had even taken place. *Had I just visited the place before time?* There was something wholesome and peaceful about it. Suddenly, a mass of blood, flesh and guts manifested from that TV frequency and became me, myself and everything. First, I was viewing it from a distance, watching it expand and swell larger than anything I could see. Before I knew it, I was a part of it, expanding with it, unfolding and tearing apart as if the universe were destroying and recreating itself over and over again, one thousand times per second. My brain felt like it was screaming, so many thoughts rushing through my feeble mind, bottlenecked as if everyone that had ever existed was speaking to me, asking me intense questions and needing answers immediately. Some of them I tried to remember:

"Does God hate me?" "I feel that I don't love my child." "Stop me from hurting myself again." I wondered if these were prayer fragments, somehow disrupting my frequency of consciousness. "Why can't I be a happy person?" "I try so fucking hard!"

Maybe the universe was telling me to rethink my problems, and that I don't have it as bad as many others. Truthfully, this all happened so quickly that I didn't have a chance to consider this possibility at the time.

My body felt like it was being ripped apart, shredded, shrunken, blown up and stretched. My consciousness wasn't in my head anymore, and it hadn't been for a while—instead, it was in front of me, revealing itself in the most hideous, hellish and horrific way possible. A giant zipper appeared amongst the sphere of flesh and skin, which was now emerging from the gigantic manifestation of this abomination. I turned my head, seeming to be in control of where to look, only to be greeted by my own family, pointing and laughing at me, then crying, upset, disgusted and heartbroken. This substantial feeling of guilt came over me, for no reason at all—as if everything that had ever happened to anybody was *my* fault. I'd been the reason for the world's failures, the world's tragedies and disgraces. The faces of my family began to melt and distort. My loved ones were being ripped away from me, torn apart and severed by some kind of invisible savage monster. It became so intense that anybody I thought of in my life would be added to this mess and split apart in the vilest, most horrifically gruesome way at the precise moment I summoned them. My parents and my brother, who were already there—completely ripped to shreds—were somehow still being sliced over and over. *Endless torture and mutilation.* Johnny and Zoe were there—I tried not to think of them but sometimes you can't be in control of where these things take you. Zoe's face melted while Johnny's face was pulled and stretched until it was shredded apart. At this time, I believed it was actually him, as if it were really happening to him. I couldn't only see his pain, but I could *feel* it. These people were all dead, whomever I'd thought of. The zipper began moving and was tearing through the fabric of reality and separating the mass of flesh into two parts and only white light was shining between them. I understood it to be nothingness—the abyss, the void. I began panicking, worried I was about to be sucked into it, never to return to my human form again, leaving the rest of the world behind and never waking up. This was death, and I was being forced to accept it.

An unspoken voice by an unseen presence communicated through my consciousness. "If you want to be cleansed, you must let go. You must *die*."

Some part of me was kicking and screaming to pull away from it, but another part of me was accepting it with all my heart, coursing towards it. That nothingness was both the representation of absolute nil, or absolutely everything in the knowing and unknowing universe combined. A long, skinny demon manifested from the rest of the flesh that had been taunting me. It was neither man nor woman, but a silhouette.

"I want to get to the white light inside your heart." It had no voice, but it spoke with intent for me to decide my fate. Even if it were talking to me without moving its lips, I knew exactly what it wanted. I let the light take me.

I woke up to the shaman holding the back of my head. I had some kind of fit, some kind of minor seizure. I instantly turned and threw up into the bucket, twice. I couldn't speak at all. I didn't know how to feel. Some thoughts began returning to me—who I was, how old I was, where I was ... even what year it was. All my senses felt as if I'd just acquired them for the first time. My vision was intensely bright, and the colours, vibrant. My hearing was distorted, yet slowly recalibrating. I could recognise the aftertaste of the tea in the back of my throat. My smell was the weakest, but I could detect some kind of incense. My hands were feeling everything as if each item were microscopic—the pillow I had beneath me felt ultra-brushy and stringy. Slowly, these senses all normalised and I was back to myself, eventually grasping the memories of what I saw, yet not quite being able to grasp it at all.

*

I waited a day or two, then headed back to the airport by the bus. I attempted to contact Johnny, who still hadn't replied to my messages or returned any of my calls. I took the next flight back to Australia but needed to make a stop in Sydney before Melbourne, to catch Zoe.

I couldn't explain my feelings after the experience, but Zoe was naturally intrigued and maybe even envious. She was just like me, just as curious and endeavoured to try ayahuasca at some point in her life. I told her it was a nightmare, but a welcomed nightmare. I wouldn't do it again, but I don't regret doing it at all. I took the lessons it gave me and thought of new ways to improve myself and understand the environments around me. *We're all connected, we're all so powerful.* It also allowed me to purge some deep and dark thoughts that'd been bottled up in my brain—some that I didn't even know I had, and some I'd rather not mention.

Only three weeks later, I received the news of Johnny's death. He overdosed in Las Vegas, no doubt from Ian and his laced crystal meth. I couldn't begin to register it. I spent months in mourning while constructing my relationship with Zoe. A massive amount of guilt had overcome me, and I realised that he would've still been alive if I hadn't dragged him on this trip with me, a trip that now felt pointless. *A meaningless death for my dearest friend.* I wasn't going to sugarcoat it. He didn't die doing what he loved. He didn't die for something worth dying for. It was all my fault, and I saw it coming. My second mistake was leaving for Peru. I should've stayed in Vegas to find him. I should've known—and I think I did know—that the 'fun' he mentioned was simply the access to his pre-abused methamphetamine.

*

A year and a half later, having been engaged to Zoe and planning the wedding, I'd spoken countless times about my guilt over Johnny. Zoe asked me if any of those psychedelics helped with the pain, guilt or self-healing. She brought salvia up for some reason—having not yet tried it. Salvia—aside from ayahuasca and datura—was one of the only substances I never wanted to experience again, and probably the most similar substance to ayahuasca/DMT in my findings. Somehow, she convinced me, possibly because I told her that I didn't regret it. Maybe it was a good chance to free myself from the pain I'd felt for a year and a half since Johnny's passing, which happened to fall on the twenty-seventh day of November. *Could the number 2711 from Johnny's datura trip have been the premonition of his fate—or, maybe even some kind of warning?*

I agreed with Zoe, that maybe it would help me understand that he'd made those decisions too and that I couldn't carry all the weight on my shoulders alone, whether it be him choosing to tag along on the trip, or abusing the drugs that he wasn't supposed to. I had endless guilt but eventually had to realise that everybody makes their own decisions regarding their own fate. Although, convincing myself of this never assisted in softening the blow.

I was able to acquire salvia from a friend of a friend who knew Fritz. I stayed in Sydney for a while and even missed out on that job opportunity as a sports journalist—but life was bigger than that now. I sat down with Zoe and let her smoke first. We weren't going to trip at the same time. This was a controlled environment, and I didn't want anything dangerous to happen during this healing process. Even though I knew salvia takes you to dark places—*the blackest*—I knew there was something waiting for me, something to confront.

"You really *are* a honeybird, you know that?" She smiled before raising the smoke-filled pipe to her lips.

"I know," I said sincerely.

After Zoe inhaled much smoother than I expected, she passed it over to me. Her body spasmed but she laughed, somewhat enjoying it and even speaking in tongues. Within a minute and a half, it was over, and she was slowly returned to reality. I took a puff, letting it absorb into my lungs. Zoe went to the bathroom to throw up as I took the second puff. It still hadn't kicked in. I was beginning to think I'd built some kind of tolerance. I took a deeper inhale ... held in maximum lung capacity for thirty seconds ... still nothing. I stood up, perplexed, suspecting an issue with the salvia, but also wondering how it affected Zoe and not me. I approached the bathroom but when I opened the door—it was empty. Zoe was nowhere to be seen. There were no windows, so she couldn't have left. The earthy scent of ayahuasca greeted my nostrils and a freshly brewed cup of dirt-coloured water sat neatly on the vanity.

"What the fuck?"

The floor slanted beneath me, and my brain warped into the cracks between the floor tiles. All I could hear was screaming. Loud, screeching, shrieking, squeals and wails. *This must've been where Zoe went.*

I woke and my vision returned. The shaman stood above me and helped me sit up. *What did I just see? What did I just experience?* This time, I didn't throw up. I cried. I couldn't help it. I was back in Peru. The shaman nodded, gesturing for me to continue crying. It was healthy and encouraged. I wept so much, helplessly and uncontrollably for any reason that I couldn't understand. *How could an entire segment of my life have been fabricated?* I sat up, regaining my senses yet again and registering where I was and what I'd just witnessed. Some part of me was exhausted, yet some part felt fresh, grounded as if I'd just awoken from a lifelong coma. I wiped my eyes and thanked the shaman, and she handed me some grapes. I couldn't believe the experience and wondered why my brain made me live through that. *There was nothing more real.* It seemed more real than reality itself. On the bus to the airport, I began to wonder and panic, worried that I'd had some kind of premonition.

What if Johnny really was dead and I was about to see Zoe and relive everything that I'd just dreamt?

What would happen in a year and a half when I take that second salvia trip? Would I wake up in Peru, once again in front of the shaman?

Is my life now stuck in this eternal loop of living the same year and a half over and over again?

Is this loop itself part of that salvia trip with Zoe? What if I'm dead? What if I'm dreaming?

I was beginning to lose my mind at the thought of it.

Your innocence, I will devour.

Your kindness, I will violate.

Your arrogance, I will dissolve.

Your honesty, I will penetrate.

Your integrity, I will consume.

Your conscience, I will manipulate.

Your patience, I will torment.

Your fate, I will orchestrate.

For you will be left with nothing but your memories, and those memories shall be all that remain.

Chapter 14

THE WAKE OF DEMISE

December 7th

I returned home, anxious that what I saw in the trip was true. Except it was quite different—immensely different. Johnny finally returned one of my calls a few days after I settled back home. *He was alive.* He hadn't responded to my calls because a week after I left for Peru, he headed straight home and sought help for his ongoing ice dependence after a short-lived relapse and a near-death experience in the hotel room of a girl named Cailee. I should have gone back for him. I should've put the pieces together. *How could I not have seen it?* As much as I regretted leaving him there, I was relieved, because a living Johnny is better than a dead one.

I planned to contact Zoe to pick up where we left off but none of my calls were returned. I knew I'd have to reconstruct the relationship I thought I had with her in my dream—since it never actually happened. Unfortunately, I didn't even get the chance.

I, instead, received a call from Fritz. "I don't know how to tell you this, Clark, but Zoe's seeing someone. His name is Jesse and she's really happy. She's the happiest I've seen her in a long time."

"Can I just get a message to her?"

After a short silence, Fritz exhaled. "It's pretty serious, Clark. I don't think it's a good idea. He's gonna ask her to marry him. *Crazy*, huh?"

"Yeah … crazy." *What else could I say? How was I supposed to feel?*

I wasn't going to break them up or interfere. Clearly, she wanted to forget about me, and I was now a part of her memory. I think I spent a little too long overseas. I felt as if I'd been gone for just over three months, even though I was aware of the dates, but even as time goes by, it may not feel like much, but a lot can happen in a year. *Eight months* I was away from home. The months must have merged into weeks that merged into days. Time dilation works both ways, experiencing lengthened periods in a short timespan like on salvia or DMT, to feeling like I'd been gone a few months, but it was closer to a year. No wonder she moved on. It turned out to be that guy she'd been messaging and ranting to me about six months earlier—she must've given in. I guess he was there, and I wasn't. I eventually concluded that if she was happy, I was—when in reality, I don't think I could ever be. That statement would only be utilised as a strategy to make me feel more content and accepting of the inalterable situation.

The vision I thought I saw in the trip was the complete opposite to the reality I was living. Johnny was alive, but

I didn't have Zoe. My mind was unable to fathom what to make of it all. *Did I live in an alternate universe for all that time? Are those things actually happening in another world and what were the aspects that caused them to differentiate from this timeline?* I had no answers, and somehow felt that anything that happened in either reality was on account of my own actions. I pondered for a few months over what I could've changed. Maybe I could have returned earlier, saved my money and attended the interview for that journalism job. Maybe I would've had Zoe waiting for me and averted any possible addiction for Johnny. A solid month earlier could have changed everything.

A year ago, this feeling would have eaten me alive. I wouldn't be able to think straight without this mass of guilt consuming me in a 'what if?' scenario. I found that after the ayahuasca, I've become more accepting of the situation around me and learned to remain at some measure of peace with whatever unfolds, whether it benefits me or not.

*

Drugs can take you to a heaven disguised as hell, or a hell disguised as heaven. It's your decision which one it will be, and whether or not to take that leap in the first place.

My advice to those curious about psychedelics is not to do it if you're looking to simply get high, get a kick out of it or if you want a buzz. You might encounter some strange, freaky and sometimes entertaining things, but these substances aren't put on this Earth just to give you any kind of joyride. Don't do them chiefly because some dickhead on a podcast told you to. Don't do them because you yearn for a thrilling high of fun shapes and colours. Do it for self-fulfilment, do it for self-discovery and exploration of your inner being. Do it to better your anxieties, work on curing your negatives and broaden your outlook on life, your surroundings and to visit the spiritual realm of who you are, your existence on Earth and the appreciation of life itself. Great benefit is found in psychedelics, discovering parts of your own brain that you never before considered, and ideas that can allow you to understand and perceive the world around you from a new, unconceived perspective. The only rule is to only do it when you're ready, when you're mentally prepared to face the innermost and darkest thoughts that reside within your psyche. Even when you think you're ready, you never will be, but at least you'll be prepared to find out. A psychedelic breakthrough will surprise you in ways you never could have imagined, but you'll thank yourself when it's all over, but only if you respect the substance and have the right intentions. If you don't, it'll sweep you right off your feet and you'll be left on your ass.

If there is one thing that I'd like to leave you with, it's the fact that energy cannot be created and it cannot be destroyed, it's always there, ever-existing, eternally transforming and morphing. These feelings and thoughts are always there, and these substances only catalyse their availability, providing us the abilities to discover and confront them. There are things to be feared, and things to be understood. The more we understand these things, the less they are to be feared. I implore you to research. I am not condoning the use of *any* drug. Every drug can be deadly if misused.

With this knowledge, I can now comprehend, to some extent, the weight of addiction through substance. Experiencing emotions—*unfelt before.* Visuals—*seen by none other.* Unsurpassed sensations of pleasure and a life that is otherwise unknown. It's easy to get lost in a substance, almost to the point where you're consumed by it—eventually forfeiting your health and wellbeing to a seal-bag of crystallised dust.

Just remember to think three times about taking any mind-altering substance, and know what high you're looking for and in what setting you're safe and comfortable to experience it in. Don't take my words as any kind of guide or definitive bible on drug-taking. This is merely a collection of my own opinionated statements and ideologies pertaining to my personal beliefs and experiences. The rest is up to you, and if you're not sure—*stay the fuck away from it.* Do your research, know your dosing limits and do not abuse any substance. Everyone's experiences are different. Your friend may have tried DMT and said he saw geometric, fractal unicorns—but you might see your own family slaughtered and mutilated beyond belief causing you a lifetime of severe trauma and anguish. Your other friend might say she survived a heavy dose of kick-ass mephedrone. *You might just die.* Question everything—and if you're not in the *right* place, or the *right* state of mind—Avoid. Any. Drug.

*

About a year later, I had almost completed my journalistic works and was soon ready for publication, rethinking the initial name for the project. *The Trip of a Lifetime* hadn't quite reflected the importance of my experience in the end, so I decided to go for something far more meaningful.

Upon many regrets during this trip, the one that seemed to stand out the most was the situation with Zoe. I was influenced by substances that I shouldn't have used, I let Johnny fall under the constriction of ice, I made that terrible mistake with Erin in Milan, I spent too long away from home, and I missed the interview for the *Sports Daily* job. But nothing weighed on my mind like Zoe. *How could I become so entrenched in the idea of someone that I'd spent such little time with?* I saw her face everywhere, I heard her name all of the time, I thought about her far more than I should have. I fucked up and I had to deal with the fact that I let her slip away. I listened to the songs that reminded me of her. I looked at the polaroids we captured together. Maybe it's these drugs that have made me seek meaning in something that's meaningless. I try to tell myself that she was just a girl I knew, finding ways of convincing myself that she was just another experience, along with all the other experiences on this trip. Maybe she was, or maybe it's my way of making myself feel better about losing one of the only people that understood me. I continued to spectate her from afar, through posted photos and word of mouth, growing, getting married, achieving her aspirations—grasping on to the faint glimmer of hope, the faint idea, the faint possibility that she'd one day return to me. The heaviest regret over this trip wasn't the fact that I'd lost her—but the fact that I'd even met her.

After the trip of trips, back home and rested, I never quite *felt* rested, I never quite settled back in. I experienced some measure of depersonalisation after trying ayahuasca. Every physical task I completed and every word I said felt as if it were performed by somebody else, some other vessel. I felt as if I were watching my life through a movie, trapped behind the glass windows of my own eyes. This frightened me for more than a few weeks until the feeling eventually escaped me without realisation. I'm still not entirely sure if it simply wore off or if I'd only gotten used to it. I still don't quite feel like myself and I don't know if I ever will.

To this day, in my dreams, I'm frequently tormented by the hallucinatory incidents caused by datura and ayahuasca—mostly the nightmarish recollections. And sometimes, during the day, the HPPD would set in—only for me, not Johnny—and I'd notice things in my line of sight like orange dots, blurs, movements and glistening diamonds on occasion. These are the payments we make for utilising some of these mystical tools.

*

I was all but finished with psychedelics and drugs at the time. I'd had enough. I received what I needed from them and documented what I'd promised. There was only one outlying issue, one question left unanswered. It bugged me, it ate at me, it kept me up at night, constantly festering and snowballing until I could no longer withstand the pressure. I knew it was something I had to confront, considering its importance in my experience with Zoe and the ayahuasca trip. *Salvia had called upon me.*

I sought out some twenty-extract sage with great difficulty. By this time, I'd forced myself to stop listening to the music I shared with Zoe, to stop looking at our photos and to stop obsessing over her life—a life that I was no longer part of. I'd achieved some sense of closure, although, it was never absolute. The salvia came at the right time. It came when I was ready for it. It was as if it'd been a part of my story and I needed to pass through it once more. It was only a matter of time before I was to approach it again.

I finally informed Johnny of my careful consideration of an additional trip down Salvia Lane, although excluding his participation—considering his recent experiences and the shitty friend I'd be to tantalise him with any kind of drug. I only informed him because I felt I owed it to him. After all, this remained *our* story, not only mine. We decided that it'd be a fitting end to this documentation. Maybe being in the mindset of this story coming to a close, Sally D might just leave us with something wise to ponder.

July 2nd

After a smooth shift at the old cafe, I headed over to Johnny's new apartment. Although I had full faith in salvia, I needed Johnny there as a trip sitter. Along with datura and ayahuasca, this was easily one of the most unpredictable substances. Salvia takes you on whatever ride it chooses, regardless of your wishes. Even if Johnny stood as a distraction, I still preferred him to be present than to do it alone and risk some kind of seizure or death. Johnny's new girlfriend was working nights, so we had the place to ourselves. In his bedroom with the doors locked and everything sharp kept safely away, I used a method of meditation to sit on the carpet and breathe slowly, focusing on each inhale and exhale. Johnny turned off the lights and only the moonlight shone through the window.

Somewhere between returning to Australia and acquiring the salvia, I obsessively researched the substance, rummaging through scientific findings, learning of the chemical compositions and listening to an abundance of trip reports. I heard similar stories to mine. The needle sensations in the chest, the squashing and slamming effect, the inability to control thoughts. There were tales of spiders crawling out of mouths, people being tangled in octopus tentacles, lips turning to playdough, scorching incineration, little elves controlling the world and the occasional haunting appearance of the user's younger selves or future kin. I even read stories of people living alternate lives for years on end, being split between dimensions and warped to unrecognisable realities—it really made me wonder why the fuck I wanted to try this stuff again.

I held the glass pipe and looked down at it, watching the sage burn into a creamy white haze. I inhaled, closing my eyes and inviting the smoke into my lungs to sit there and burn for a while. Familiar in its way—it was warm and alluring, as if Salvia's silk cloak had already begun to embrace me. She knew I'd be returning to her. I thought about the time I was trapped in the wrong reality, and how I believed I was trying salvia with Zoe, but it was just a trip. I needed to relax my brain and halt thoughts about anything that might be excessively strenuous on the mind, especially about a reality that didn't happen, or may have happened in another universe, or even a reality that I connected with on a spiritual plane. Any rogue thought could affect this experience far beyond belief. *Another puff ought to do it.*

I inhaled once more.

GLOSSARY

DELIRIANT: A subclass of hallucinogen. A substance capable of inducing acute delirium, commonly associated with restlessness or agitation.

DEPERSONALISATION: A state in which one's thoughts and feelings seem unreal or not to belong to oneself.

DISSOCIATION: The action of disconnecting or separating, or the state of being disconnected.

EMPATHOGEN: Substances that cause the brain to release dopamine and serotonin. They can increase feelings of connection and empathy, pleasure and energy levels but can also cause mood swings, dehydration and depression.

EGO-DEATH: The demise of your sense of self. Ego death results in a significant reduction of self-referential awareness, sparking a disruption in how you view yourself in the world.

HPPD (Hallucinogen Persisting Perception Disorder): Encompassing a range of mostly visual perceptual disturbances that occur within a certain time frame after cessation of drug use.

INHALANT: Volatile substances that produce chemical vapours that can be inhaled to induce a psychoactive, or mind-altering, effect.

INTRAVENOUS: Administering a substance through a needle or tube inserted into a vein. Also called IV.

INTROSPECTION: A psychological process that involves looking inward to examine one's own thoughts, emotions, judgements and perceptions.

K-HOLE (SLANG): Ketamine induces dose-related effects that include distortion of time and space, hallucinations and mild dissociative effects. During a 'k-hole', users experience an enhanced detachment from the environment, resulting in an inability to respond to surroundings and move functionally.

MICRODOSING: The action or practice of taking or administering very small amounts of a drug in order to test or benefit from its physiological action while minimising undesirable side effects.

MICROPSIA: A condition in which visual objects are perceived to be smaller than they are objectively sized.

NARCOTICS: Used to treat moderate to severe pain.

OPIOID: A class of drugs that derive from, or mimic, natural substances found in the opium poppy plant. Opioids work in the brain to produce a variety of effects, including pain relief.

PERMA-FRIED (SLANG): Permanently experiencing the effects of, or suffering permanent psychological damage as a result of prolonged or intense use of psychoactive drugs.

POLYDRUG USE: The use of more than one drug or type of drug at the same time or one after another. Can be referred to as 'cross-faded' for slang.

PSYCHEDELIC: Substances that produce changes in perception, mood and cognitive processes.

PSYCHOACTIVE: A drug or other substance that affects how the brain works and causes changes in mood, awareness, thoughts, feelings or behaviour.

PSYCHONAUT (SLANG): Someone who explores altered states of consciousness, especially through hallucinatory drugs.

STIMULANT: A substance that raises levels of physiological or nervous activity in the body.

SUBLINGUAL: The pharmacological route of administration by which substances diffuse into the blood through tissues under the tongue.

ACKNOWLEDGEMENTS

No novel is complete without the assistance of some incredible individuals. Even the most solitary writers require someone to rely on during at least one stage of the process. There are many I wish I could thank, but by thanking them, I'd have to thank about a hundred other people ... and by thanking those hundred, the next thousand would be asking why they weren't thanked. Unfortunately, this list would go on and on if I named everybody and their best friend. I'd rather keep it simple.

The first piece of appreciation would be to my dear readers: Anybody that spared a mere second of their lives to glance upon this book, pick it up, borrow it, purchase it, skim through it—or in the rare instance—*actually read the damn thing*—thank you for giving my words your time. I hope to have more for you soon.

***

To my lovely wife, thank you for being so patient and supportive with me and this book—I know it's a strange subject to base my debut novel on. Your presence in my life is invaluable and I'll forever appreciate and cherish you.
To my family: My father, my sisters, my grandparents, my brothers-in-law, my sister-in-law, and my parents-in-law. I am *so* glad, and *so* lucky to have people like you in my life to lean on, call upon, seek advice from and vent to. I often wonder what I'd do without this support around me, and realise that many others aren't blessed with amazing people like these—I must constantly remind myself not to take this gift for granted.

To Aidan, you are my best friend in the world, and my best man. Your input on the first manuscript of *Honeybird* provided me with a new perspective on the book and way to enhance and improve it. I can't thank you enough for that. Thank you also for the stories. The stories from the past, and the stories that are yet to be lived.

To Dilhan—for reasons needn't to be explained. *Thank you.*

To Marco, for the ongoing support, advice and dealing with my constantly fluctuating moods during the writing process—which can be a real pain in the ass. Thank you for enduring me, motivating me and being there always.

To my proofreader, Anita. Thank you for being so concise, thorough and easy to work with. The gears work better when these in-between jobs are a breeze.

To my cover designer, Anze. Working together on the book design resulted in exactly what I'd envisioned. Your creativity and professionalism is much appreciated, and I hope to collaborate again soon.

***

And finally, mostly, and deservedly: My mother. The one who understands me without judgement. The one who lends a hand in any situation, whether she has a full plate or not. No matter how stressed she is, puts everything aside to assist those in need, giving more than she ever has to give. Without you, I wouldn't be so in love with poetry and storytelling. You are the origin, the ignition and the catalyst to my growth as a writer. I can't possibly be more thankful. So much of my work, refinements and motivation is credited to you, even when things are difficult to say—and constructive criticism being a kick in the teeth—you won't beat around the bush because you know it's for the greater good, believing I won't crumble, but flourish. Thank you, Mum.

"A bird in the hand is worth two in the bush."

ABOUT THE AUTHOR

Born in Melbourne, Australia, Rafael Francis wrote *Honeybird* at the age of twenty-four and had it published at twenty-five. In the six years prior, Rafael had been writing screenplays for film and television, gaining a taste for storytelling under a heavily restricted format, and received a number of accolades for his works as a screenwriter.

Rafael's switch to writing novels came as a fresh and enlightening change. Writing with unshackled creativity and restriction compared to that of screenwriting, Rafael found it to be a freeing experience, not only writing for the audience, but for himself.

Rafael Francis is well known to articulate his stories in a manner that is easy to visualise. Timespans in his scripts and novels are known to dilate and slow down, almost to a momentary halt—or speed up, to the passing of three months in a single sentence. A common trend with Rafael's writing is the bittersweetness. He likes to remind his audience that the protagonists don't always win, and the most villainous characters don't always fall. It's the realities of life and knowing that every story isn't always a three-act fairy tale.

"There is no *correct* way to write. Creation has no rules and knows no bounds. If I can impact my intended audience—make them feel something, then I consider my purpose fulfilled."
-*Rafael Francis*

OUT NOW

Honeybird: Lucid Edition illustrated by Rita H Rowe

INCLUDES:

- 20+ hand-drawn charcoal illustrations by artist and novelist – Rita H Rowe
- Bonus content: exclusive notes, quotes and anecdotes by Rafael Francis
- New 7"x10" size special edition
- High-quality gloss finish hardcover
- Premium white page interior

Rita H Rowe's illustrations are inspired by the twisted and intoxicatingly unhinged reflections of Clark Burrows in Honeybird. Clark and Johnny's manic, philosophic and dream-like retrospective encounters are perfectly represented in raw, unbounded charcoal by Rowe to convey expression and visual depth to the original Honeybird narrative.